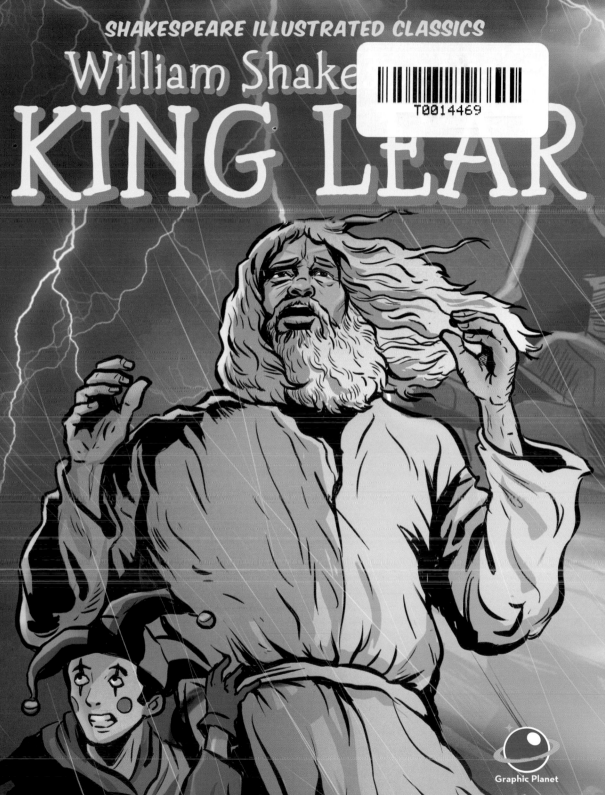

SHAKESPEARE ILLUSTRATED CLASSICS

William Shake[speare]
KING LEAR

T0014469

Graphic Planet

An Imprint of Magic Wagon
abdobooks.com

abdobooks.com

Published by Magic Wagon, a division of ABDO, PO Box 398166, Minneapolis, Minnesota 55439. Copyright © 2023 by Abdo Consulting Group, Inc. International copyrights reserved in all countries. No part of this book may be reproduced in any form without written permission from the publisher. Graphic Planet™ is a trademark and logo of Magic Wagon.

Printed in the United States of America, North Mankato, Minnesota.
052022
092022

THIS BOOK CONTAINS
RECYCLED MATERIALS

Adapted by Daniel Conner and Brian Farrens
Cover art by Dave Shephard
Interior art by Ben Dunn
Edited by Tamara L. Britton
Interior layout and design by Candice Keimig and Colleen McLaren

Library of Congress Control Number: 2021951986

Publisher's Cataloging-in-Publication Data

Names: Shakespeare, William; Conner, Daniel; Farrens, Brian, authors. | Dunn, Ben, illustrator.
Title: William Shakespeare's King Lear / by William Shakespeare, Adapted by Daniel Conner and Brian Farrens; illustrated by Ben Dunn.
Description: Minneapolis, Minnesota: Magic Wagon, 2023. | Series: Shakespeare illustrated classics
Summary: As King Lear tries to split his kingdom among his three daughters, the chaos and mistrust that ensue drive him mad.
Identifiers: ISBN 9781098233280 (lib. bdg.) | ISBN 9781644948422 (pbk.) | ISBN 9781098234126 (ebook) | ISBN 9781098234546 (Read-to-Me ebook)
Subjects: LCSH: King Lear (Shakespeare, William)--Juvenile fiction. | Lear, King of England (Legendary character)--Juvenile fiction. | Tragedy--Juvenile fiction. | Kings and rulers--Juvenile fiction. | Fathers and daughters--Juvenile fiction. | Inheritance and succession--Juvenile fiction. | Literature--Juvenile fiction.
Classification: DDC 741.5--dc23

Table of Contents

Cast of Characters

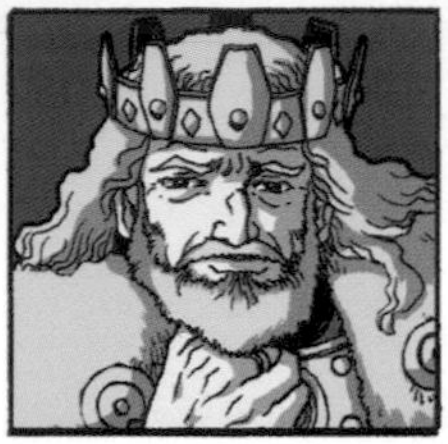

KING LEAR
King of Britain

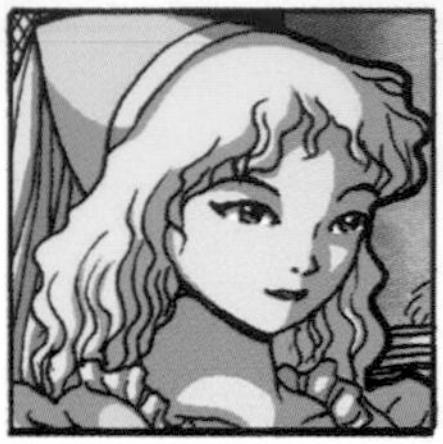

GONERIL
Lear's eldest daughter

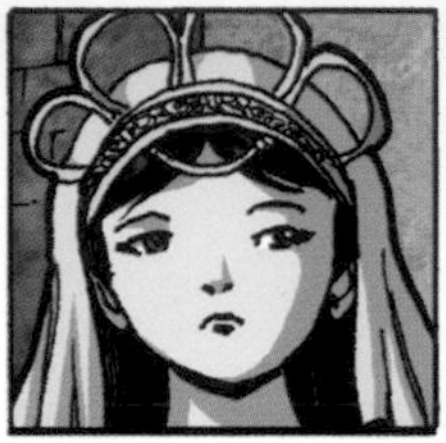

REGAN
Lear's second-eldest daughter

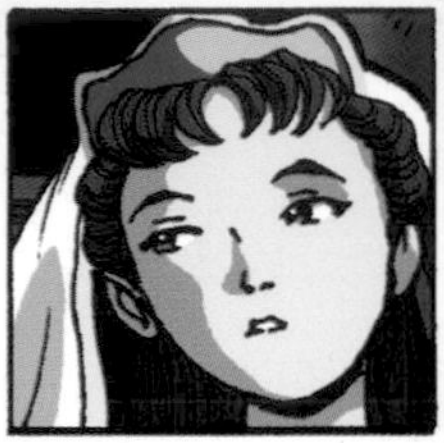

CORDELIA
Lear's youngest daughter

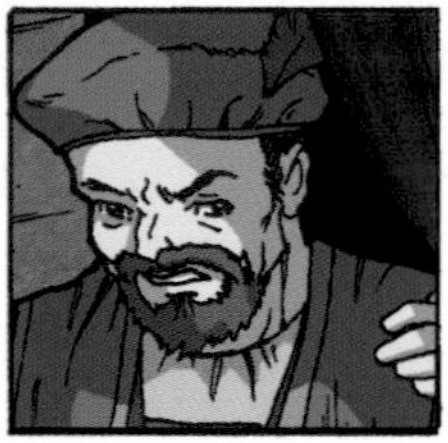

ALBANY
Duke of Albany, Goneril's husband

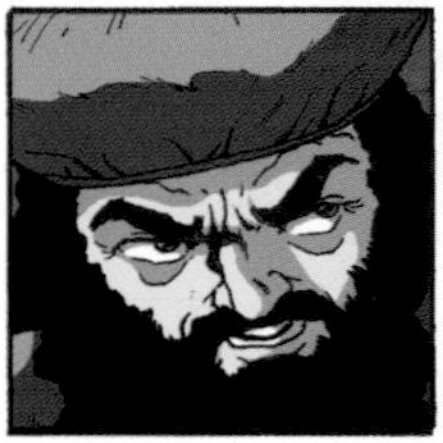

CORNWALL
Duke of Cornwall, Regan's husband

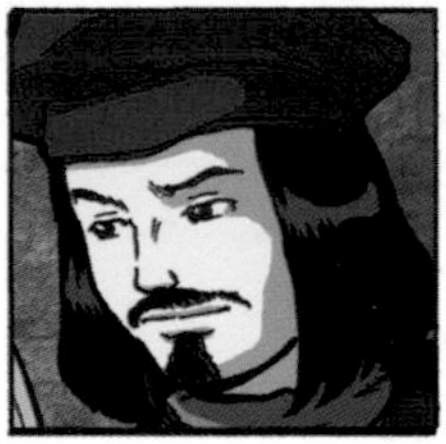

FRANCE
King of France, Cordelia's husband

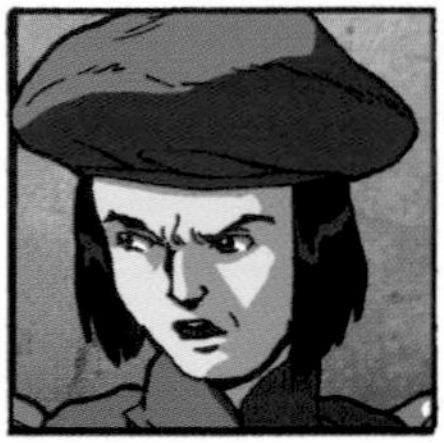

GLOUCESTER
Father of Edgar and Edmund

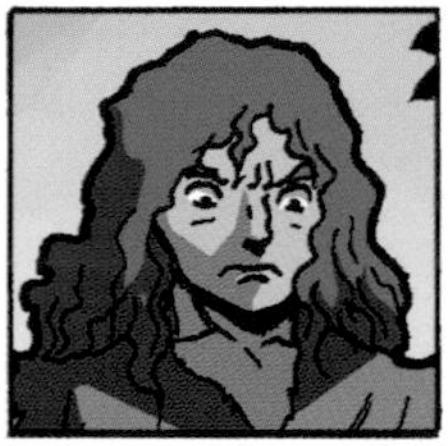

EDGAR
Gloucester's legitimate son

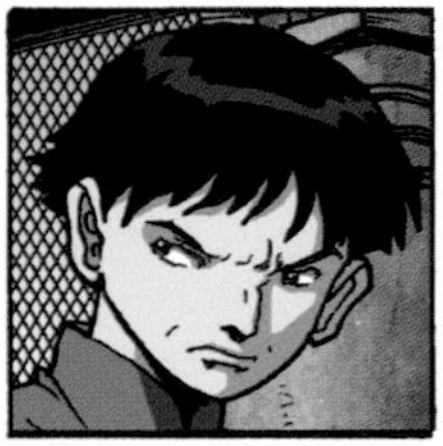

EDMUND
Gloucester's illegitimate son

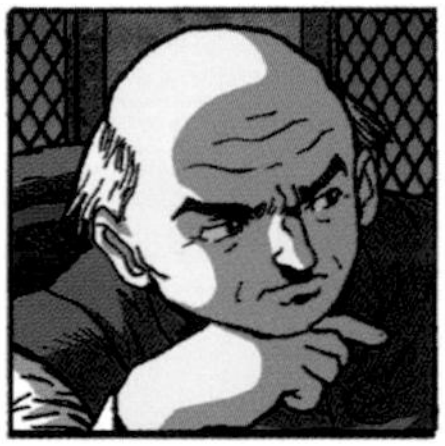

KENT
Earl of Kent

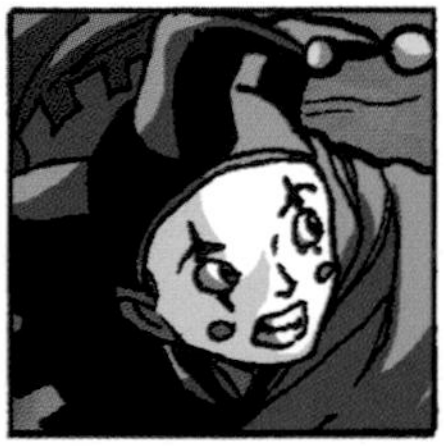

FOOL
King Lear's court jester

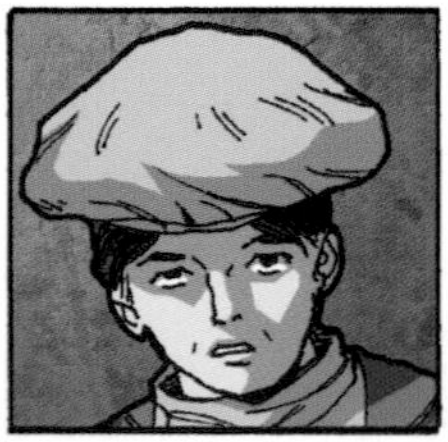

OSWALD
Goneril's servant

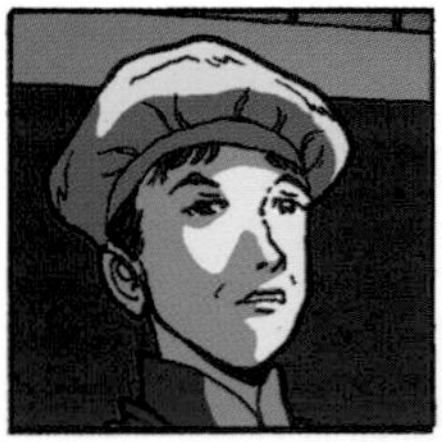

GENTLEMAN
An attendant to Kent and Edgar

Synopsis

King Lear is nearing the end of his reign. Before he steps down, he decides to divide his kingdom between his three daughters Goneril, Regan, and Cordelia. To determine how his wealth will be split among the three, Lear asks each how much she loves him. Goneril and Regan flatter Lear with exaggerated proclamations of love. Cordelia remains silent.

King Lear, enraged at his youngest and favorite daughter, disowns her, and Cordelia leaves the kingdom for France, where she is to marry the king. Soon, Lear sees what he has done when Goneril and Regan begin to betray their father and slowly goes insane. He goes out with his fool and Kent and encounters a thunderstorm.

Meanwhile, Gloucester, a loyal nobleman, decides to help Lear. But Regan and her husband Cornwall accuse Gloucester of treason, blind him, and turn him out to roam the land. His legitimate son, Edgar, disguised as a beggar, leads him to Dover, where King Lear has ended up.

Cordelia arrives in Dover with a French army to save King Lear. But the English army, led by Gloucester's illegitimate son Edmund, arrives and defeats the French forces. Cordelia and Lear are imprisoned. Edgar kills Edmund in a duel. Goneril poisons Regan then kills herself when her husband Albany learns of her deed. Cordelia is executed in prison, and Lear dies of grief.

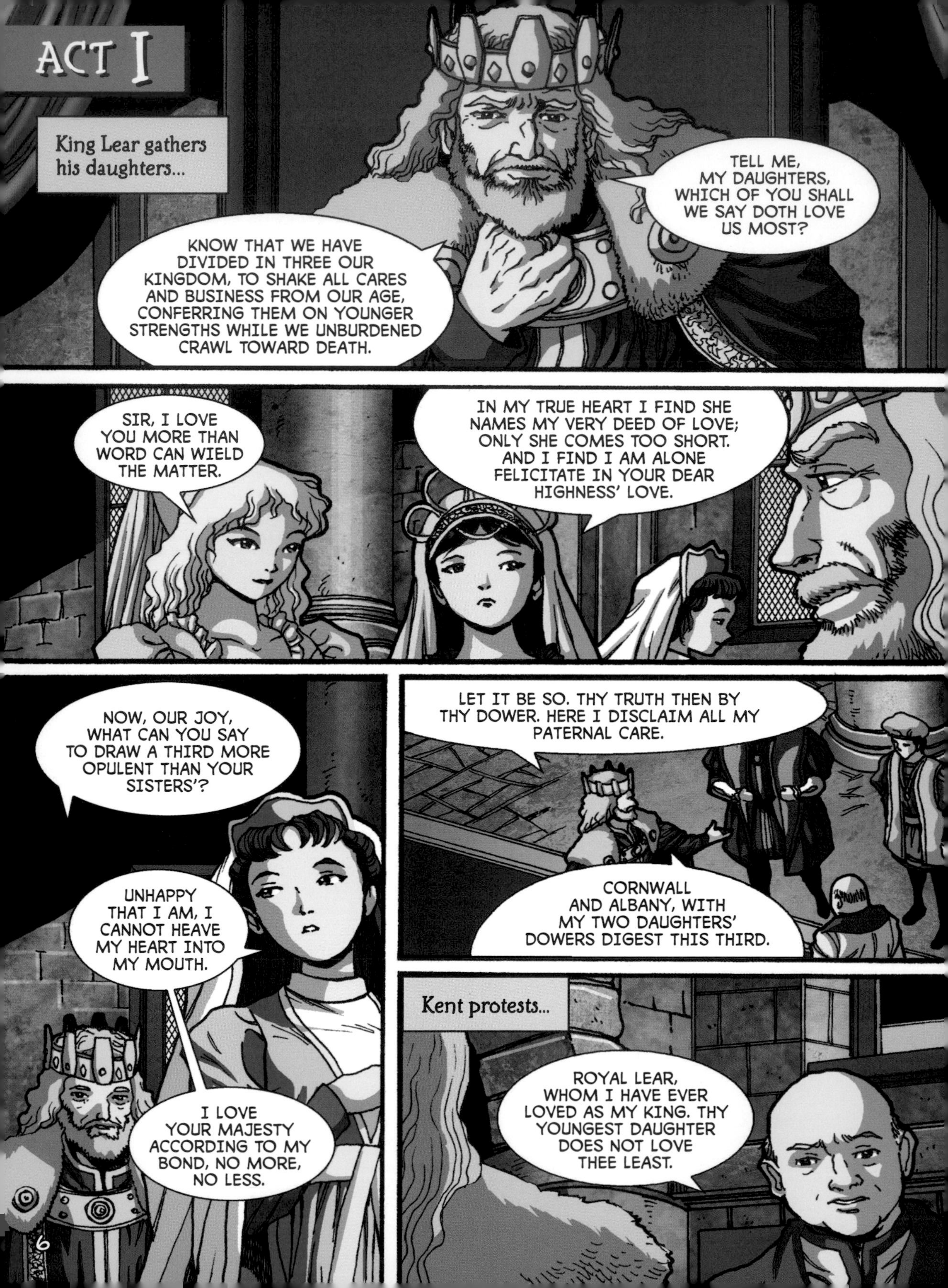
ACT I
King Lear gathers his daughters...
KNOW THAT WE HAVE DIVIDED IN THREE OUR KINGDOM, TO SHAKE ALL CARES AND BUSINESS FROM OUR AGE, CONFERRING THEM ON YOUNGER STRENGTHS WHILE WE UNBURDENED CRAWL TOWARD DEATH.
TELL ME, MY DAUGHTERS, WHICH OF YOU SHALL WE SAY DOTH LOVE US MOST?
SIR, I LOVE YOU MORE THAN WORD CAN WIELD THE MATTER.
IN MY TRUE HEART I FIND SHE NAMES MY VERY DEED OF LOVE; ONLY SHE COMES TOO SHORT. AND I FIND I AM ALONE FELICITATE IN YOUR DEAR HIGHNESS' LOVE.
NOW, OUR JOY, WHAT CAN YOU SAY TO DRAW A THIRD MORE OPULENT THAN YOUR SISTERS'?
UNHAPPY THAT I AM, I CANNOT HEAVE MY HEART INTO MY MOUTH.
I LOVE YOUR MAJESTY ACCORDING TO MY BOND, NO MORE, NO LESS.
LET IT BE SO. THY TRUTH THEN BY THY DOWER. HERE I DISCLAIM ALL MY PATERNAL CARE.
CORNWALL AND ALBANY, WITH MY TWO DAUGHTERS' DOWERS DIGEST THIS THIRD.
Kent protests...
ROYAL LEAR, WHOM I HAVE EVER LOVED AS MY KING. THY YOUNGEST DAUGHTER DOES NOT LOVE THEE LEAST.

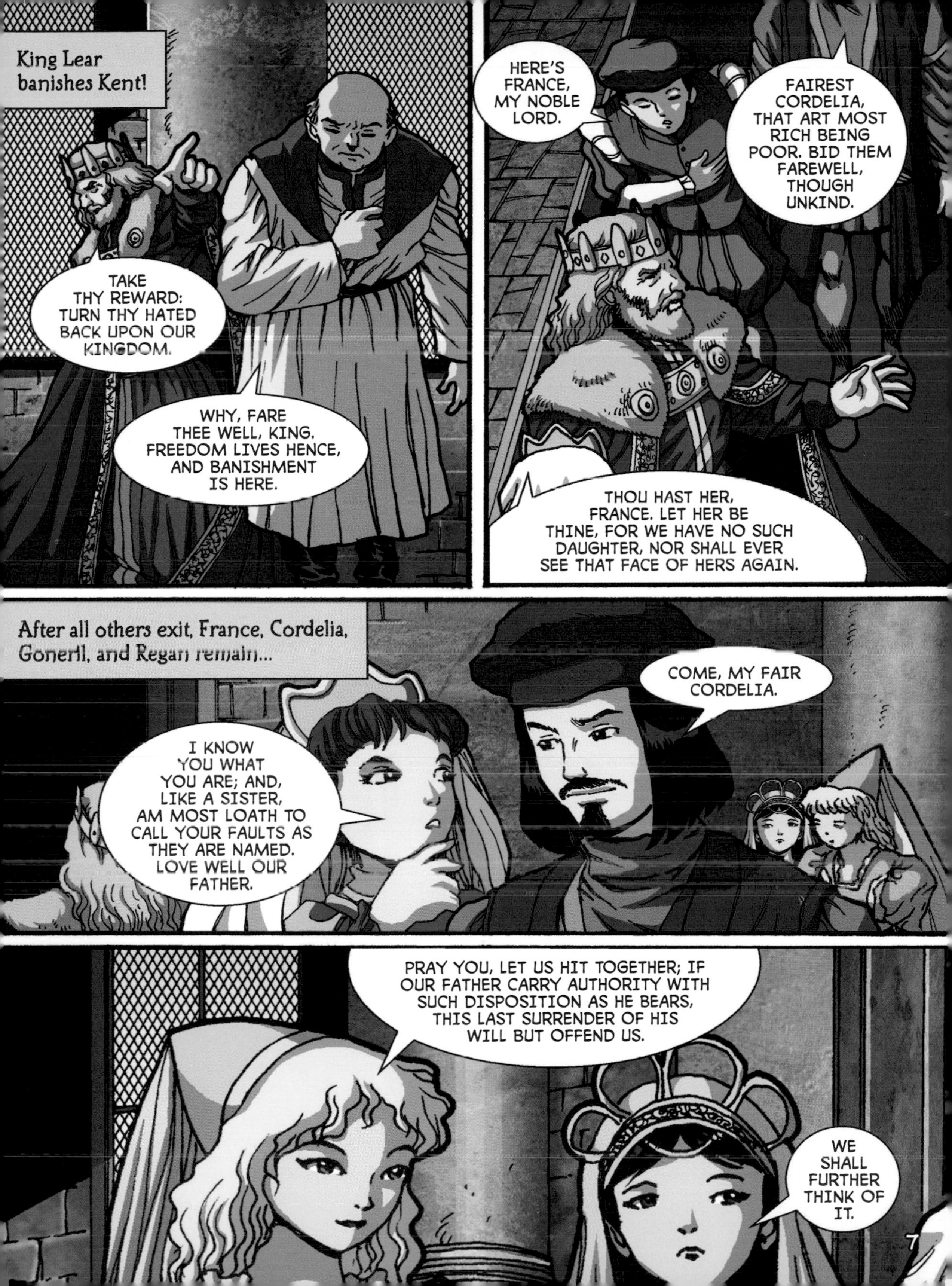
King Lear banishes Kent!
TAKE THY REWARD: TURN THY HATED BACK UPON OUR KINGDOM.
WHY, FARE THEE WELL, KING. FREEDOM LIVES HENCE, AND BANISHMENT IS HERE.
HERE'S FRANCE, MY NOBLE LORD.
FAIREST CORDELIA, THAT ART MOST RICH BEING POOR. BID THEM FAREWELL, THOUGH UNKIND.
THOU HAST HER, FRANCE. LET HER BE THINE, FOR WE HAVE NO SUCH DAUGHTER, NOR SHALL EVER SEE THAT FACE OF HERS AGAIN.
After all others exit, France, Cordelia, Goneril, and Regan remain...
COME, MY FAIR CORDELIA.
I KNOW YOU WHAT YOU ARE; AND, LIKE A SISTER, AM MOST LOATH TO CALL YOUR FAULTS AS THEY ARE NAMED. LOVE WELL OUR FATHER.
PRAY YOU, LET US HIT TOGETHER; IF OUR FATHER CARRY AUTHORITY WITH SUCH DISPOSITION AS HE BEARS, THIS LAST SURRENDER OF HIS WILL BUT OFFEND US.
WE SHALL FURTHER THINK OF IT.

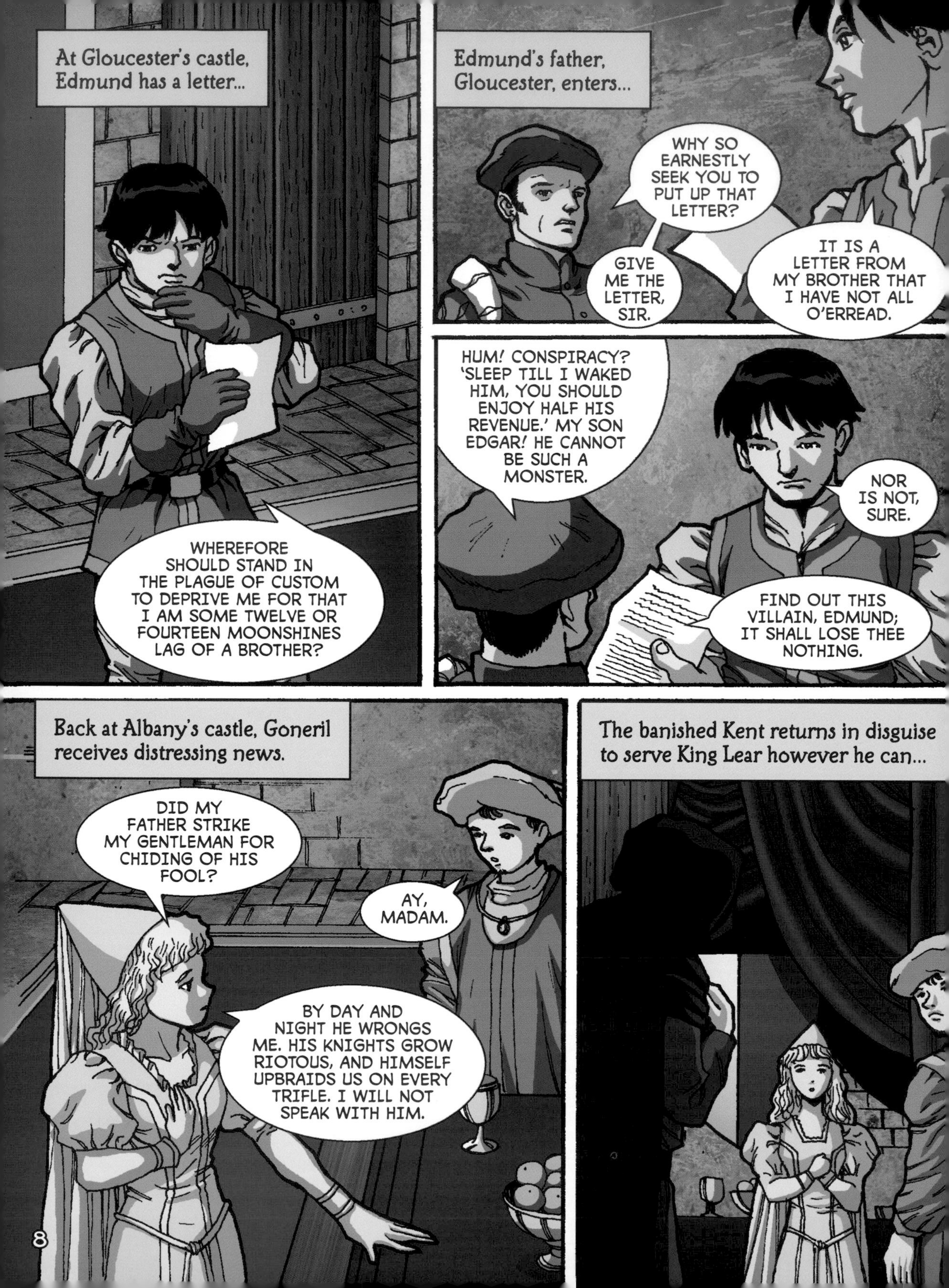
At Gloucester's castle, Edmund has a letter...
WHEREFORE SHOULD STAND IN THE PLAGUE OF CUSTOM TO DEPRIVE ME FOR THAT I AM SOME TWELVE OR FOURTEEN MOONSHINES LAG OF A BROTHER?
Edmund's father, Gloucester, enters...
WHY SO EARNESTLY SEEK YOU TO PUT UP THAT LETTER?
IT IS A LETTER FROM MY BROTHER THAT I HAVE NOT ALL O'ERREAD.
GIVE ME THE LETTER, SIR.
HUM! CONSPIRACY? 'SLEEP TILL I WAKED HIM, YOU SHOULD ENJOY HALF HIS REVENUE.' MY SON EDGAR! HE CANNOT BE SUCH A MONSTER.
NOR IS NOT, SURE.
FIND OUT THIS VILLAIN, EDMUND; IT SHALL LOSE THEE NOTHING.
Back at Albany's castle, Goneril receives distressing news.
DID MY FATHER STRIKE MY GENTLEMAN FOR CHIDING OF HIS FOOL?
AY, MADAM.
BY DAY AND NIGHT HE WRONGS ME. HIS KNIGHTS GROW RIOTOUS, AND HIMSELF UPBRAIDS US ON EVERY TRIFLE. I WILL NOT SPEAK WITH HIM.
The banished Kent returns in disguise to serve King Lear however he can...

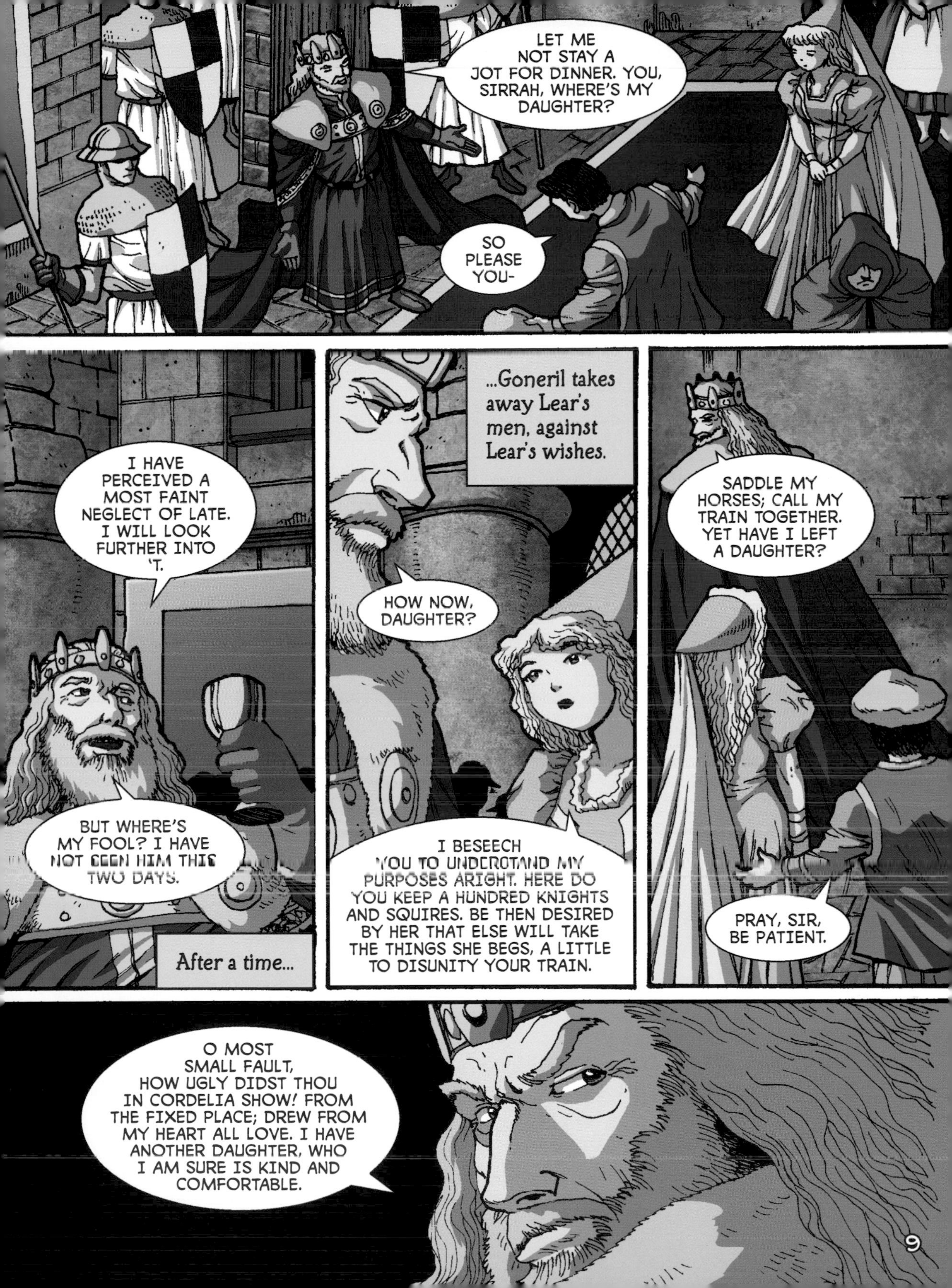
LET ME NOT STAY A JOT FOR DINNER. YOU, SIRRAH, WHERE'S MY DAUGHTER?
SO PLEASE YOU-
I HAVE PERCEIVED A MOST FAINT NEGLECT OF LATE. I WILL LOOK FURTHER INTO 'T.
BUT WHERE'S MY FOOL? I HAVE NOT SEEN HIM THIS TWO DAYS.
After a time...
...Goneril takes away Lear's men, against Lear's wishes.
HOW NOW, DAUGHTER?
I BESEECH YOU TO UNDERSTAND MY PURPOSES ARIGHT. HERE DO YOU KEEP A HUNDRED KNIGHTS AND SQUIRES. BE THEN DESIRED BY HER THAT ELSE WILL TAKE THE THINGS SHE BEGS, A LITTLE TO DISUNITY YOUR TRAIN.
SADDLE MY HORSES; CALL MY TRAIN TOGETHER. YET HAVE I LEFT A DAUGHTER?
PRAY, SIR, BE PATIENT.
O MOST SMALL FAULT, HOW UGLY DIDST THOU IN CORDELIA SHOW! FROM THE FIXED PLACE; DREW FROM MY HEART ALL LOVE. I HAVE ANOTHER DAUGHTER, WHO I AM SURE IS KIND AND COMFORTABLE.

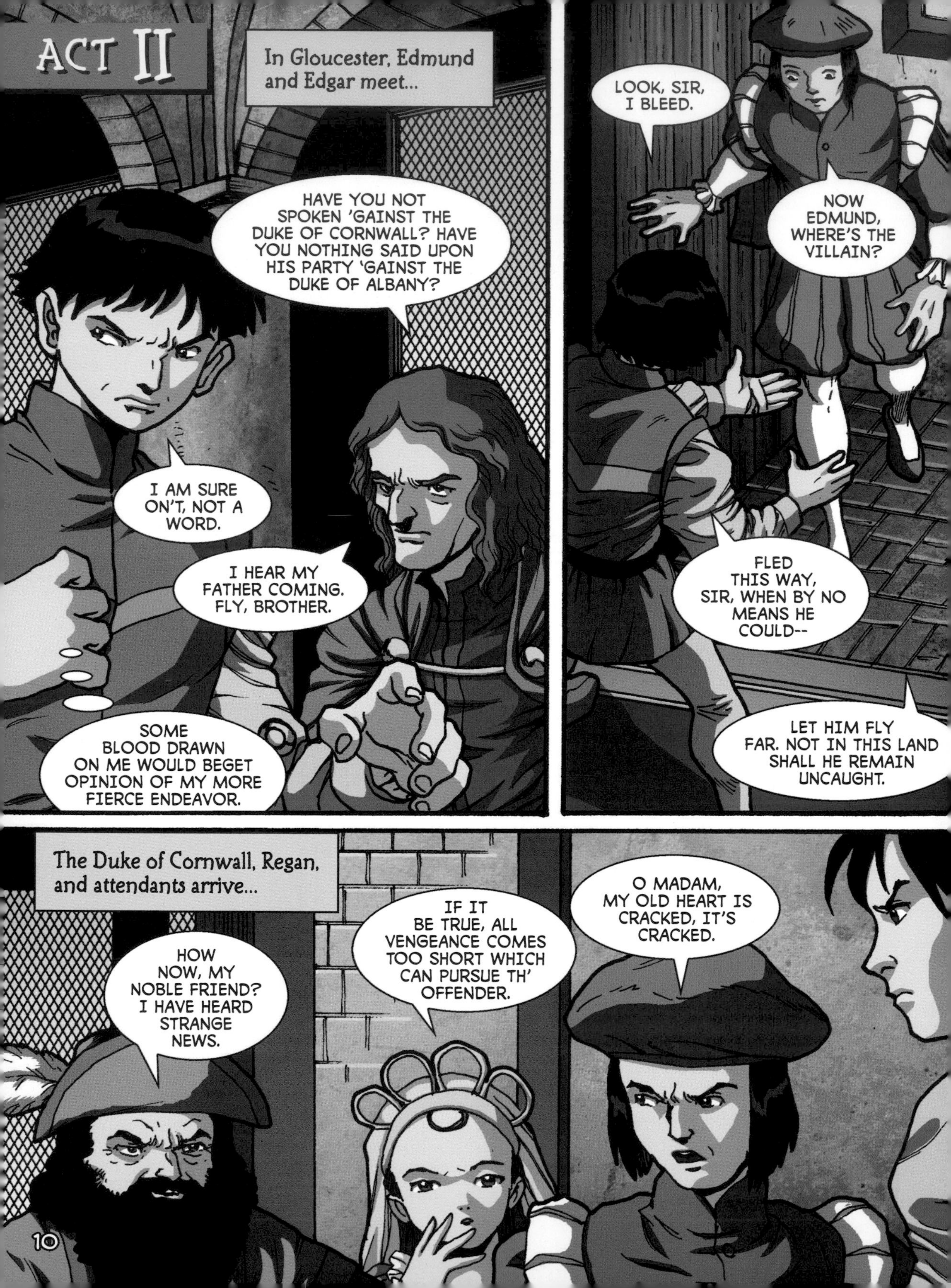
ACT II
In Gloucester, Edmund and Edgar meet...
HAVE YOU NOT SPOKEN 'GAINST THE DUKE OF CORNWALL? HAVE YOU NOTHING SAID UPON HIS PARTY 'GAINST THE DUKE OF ALBANY?
I AM SURE ON'T, NOT A WORD.
I HEAR MY FATHER COMING. FLY, BROTHER.
SOME BLOOD DRAWN ON ME WOULD BEGET OPINION OF MY MORE FIERCE ENDEAVOR.
LOOK, SIR, I BLEED.
NOW EDMUND, WHERE'S THE VILLAIN?
FLED THIS WAY, SIR, WHEN BY NO MEANS HE COULD--
LET HIM FLY FAR. NOT IN THIS LAND SHALL HE REMAIN UNCAUGHT.
The Duke of Cornwall, Regan, and attendants arrive...
HOW NOW, MY NOBLE FRIEND? I HAVE HEARD STRANGE NEWS.
IF IT BE TRUE, ALL VENGEANCE COMES TOO SHORT WHICH CAN PURSUE TH' OFFENDER.
O MADAM, MY OLD HEART IS CRACKED, IT'S CRACKED.

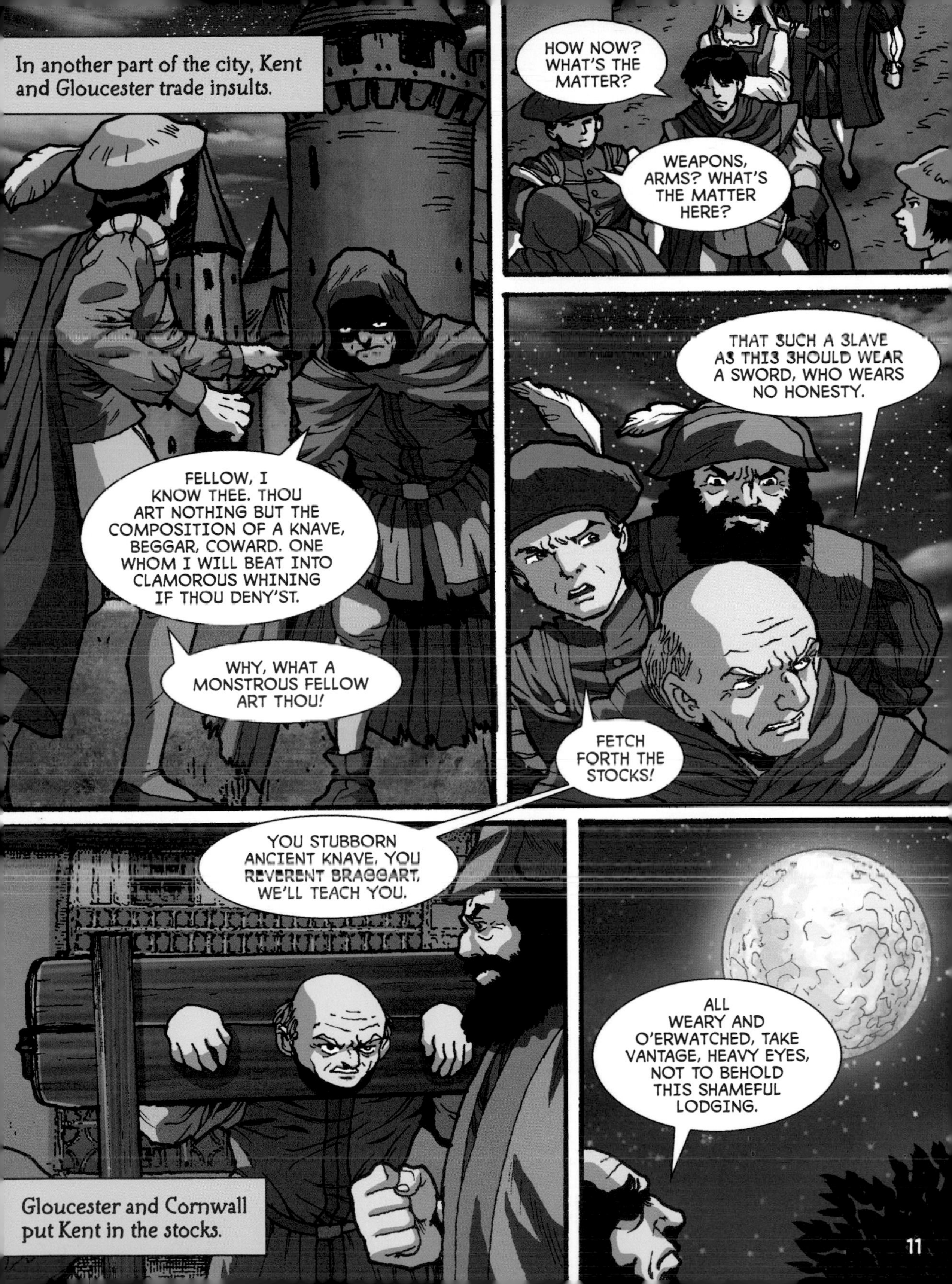
In another part of the city, Kent and Gloucester trade insults.
HOW NOW? WHAT'S THE MATTER?
WEAPONS, ARMS? WHAT'S THE MATTER HERE?
FELLOW, I KNOW THEE. THOU ART NOTHING BUT THE COMPOSITION OF A KNAVE, BEGGAR, COWARD. ONE WHOM I WILL BEAT INTO CLAMOROUS WHINING IF THOU DENY'ST.
WHY, WHAT A MONSTROUS FELLOW ART THOU!
THAT SUCH A SLAVE AS THIS SHOULD WEAR A SWORD, WHO WEARS NO HONESTY.
FETCH FORTH THE STOCKS!
YOU STUBBORN ANCIENT KNAVE, YOU REVERENT BRAGGART, WE'LL TEACH YOU.
Gloucester and Cornwall put Kent in the stocks.
ALL WEARY AND O'ERWATCHED, TAKE VANTAGE, HEAVY EYES, NOT TO BEHOLD THIS SHAMEFUL LODGING.

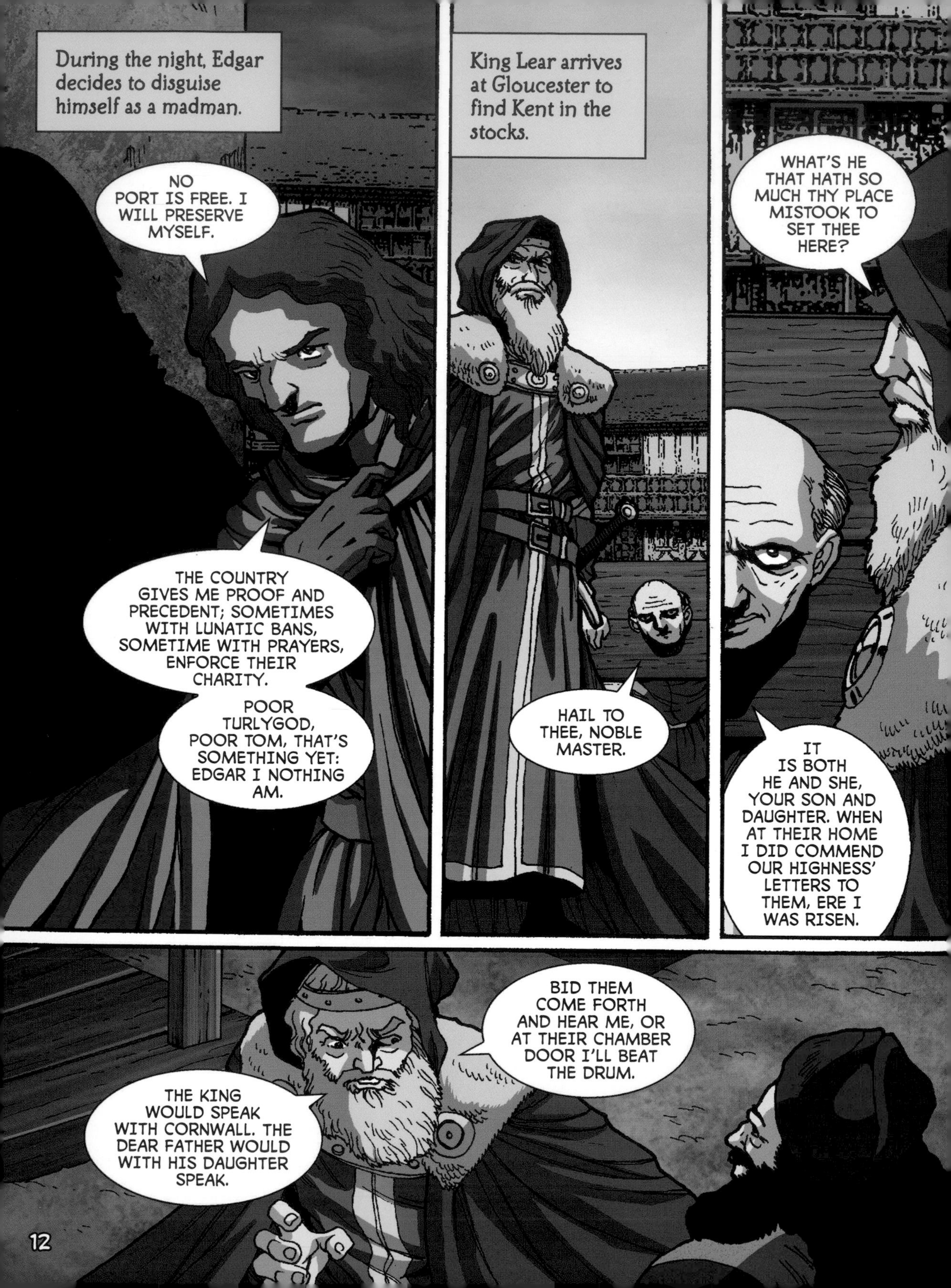

During the night, Edgar decides to disguise himself as a madman.
NO PORT IS FREE. I WILL PRESERVE MYSELF.
THE COUNTRY GIVES ME PROOF AND PRECEDENT; SOMETIMES WITH LUNATIC BANS, SOMETIME WITH PRAYERS, ENFORCE THEIR CHARITY.
POOR TURLYGOD, POOR TOM, THAT'S SOMETHING YET: EDGAR I NOTHING AM.
King Lear arrives at Gloucester to find Kent in the stocks.
HAIL TO THEE, NOBLE MASTER.
WHAT'S HE THAT HATH SO MUCH THY PLACE MISTOOK TO SET THEE HERE?
IT IS BOTH HE AND SHE, YOUR SON AND DAUGHTER. WHEN AT THEIR HOME I DID COMMEND OUR HIGHNESS' LETTERS TO THEM, ERE I WAS RISEN.
THE KING WOULD SPEAK WITH CORNWALL. THE DEAR FATHER WOULD WITH HIS DAUGHTER SPEAK.
BID THEM COME FORTH AND HEAR ME, OR AT THEIR CHAMBER DOOR I'LL BEAT THE DRUM.

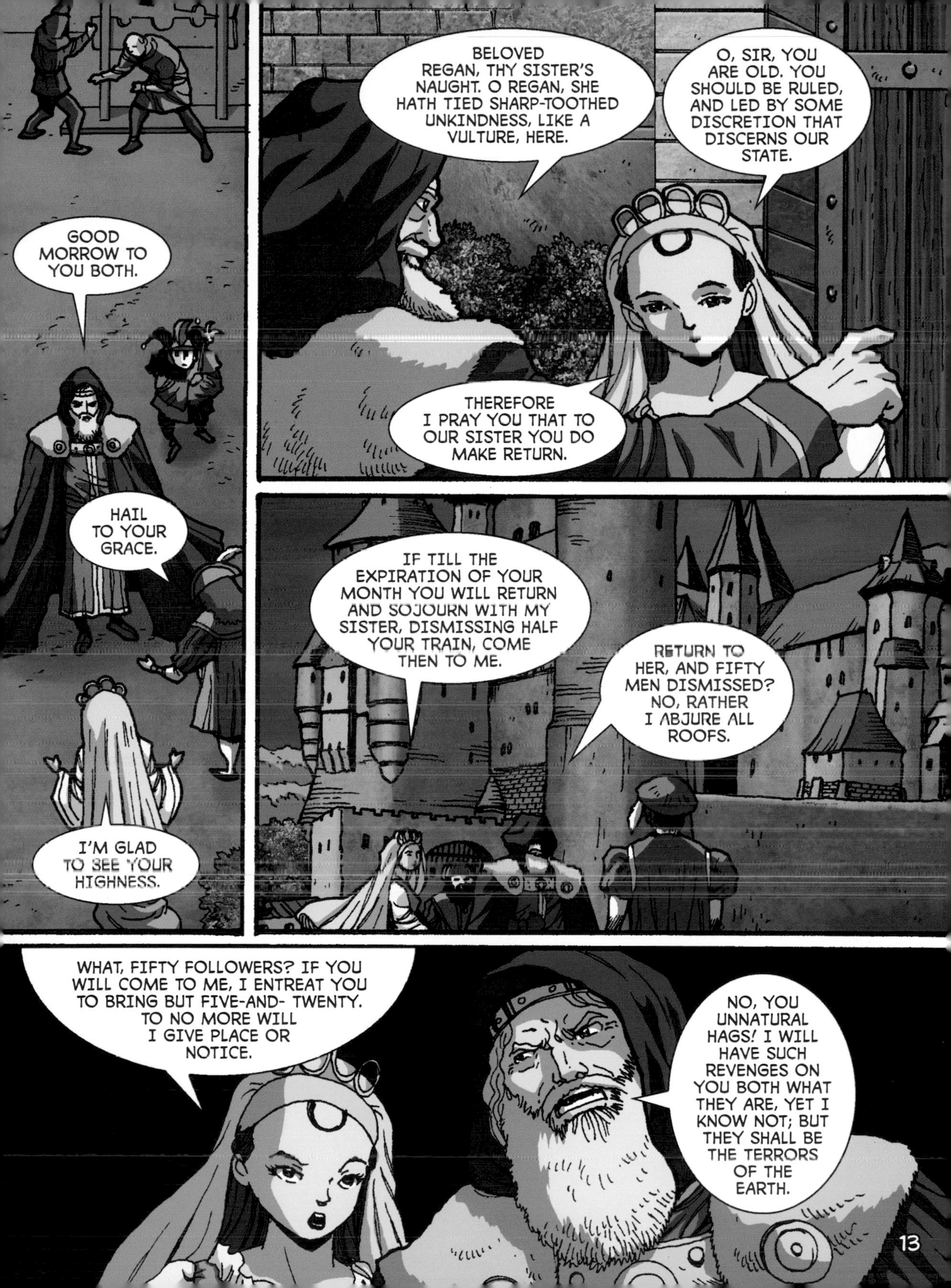
GOOD MORROW TO YOU BOTH.
HAIL TO YOUR GRACE.
I'M GLAD TO SEE YOUR HIGHNESS.
BELOVED REGAN, THY SISTER'S NAUGHT. O REGAN, SHE HATH TIED SHARP-TOOTHED UNKINDNESS, LIKE A VULTURE, HERE.
O, SIR, YOU ARE OLD. YOU SHOULD BE RULED, AND LED BY SOME DISCRETION THAT DISCERNS OUR STATE.
THEREFORE I PRAY YOU THAT TO OUR SISTER YOU DO MAKE RETURN.
IF TILL THE EXPIRATION OF YOUR MONTH YOU WILL RETURN AND SOJOURN WITH MY SISTER, DISMISSING HALF YOUR TRAIN, COME THEN TO ME.
RETURN TO HER, AND FIFTY MEN DISMISSED? NO, RATHER I ABJURE ALL ROOFS.
WHAT, FIFTY FOLLOWERS? IF YOU WILL COME TO ME, I ENTREAT YOU TO BRING BUT FIVE-AND- TWENTY. TO NO MORE WILL I GIVE PLACE OR NOTICE.
NO, YOU UNNATURAL HAGS! I WILL HAVE SUCH REVENGES ON YOU BOTH WHAT THEY ARE, YET I KNOW NOT; BUT THEY SHALL BE THE TERRORS OF THE EARTH.

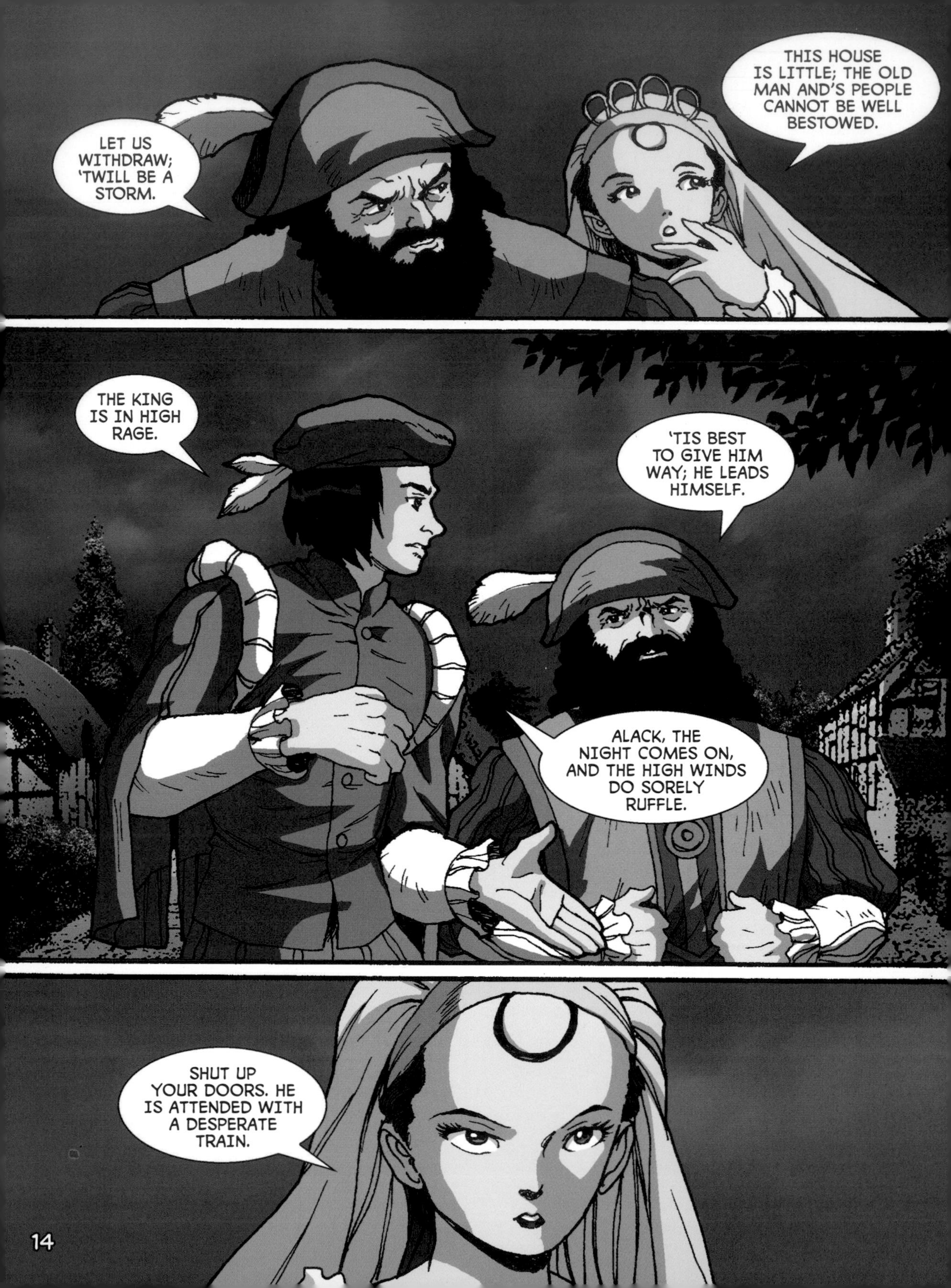
LET US WITHDRAW; 'TWILL BE A STORM.
THIS HOUSE IS LITTLE; THE OLD MAN AND'S PEOPLE CANNOT BE WELL BESTOWED.
THE KING IS IN HIGH RAGE.
'TIS BEST TO GIVE HIM WAY; HE LEADS HIMSELF.
ALACK, THE NIGHT COMES ON, AND THE HIGH WINDS DO SORELY RUFFLE.
SHUT UP YOUR DOORS. HE IS ATTENDED WITH A DESPERATE TRAIN.

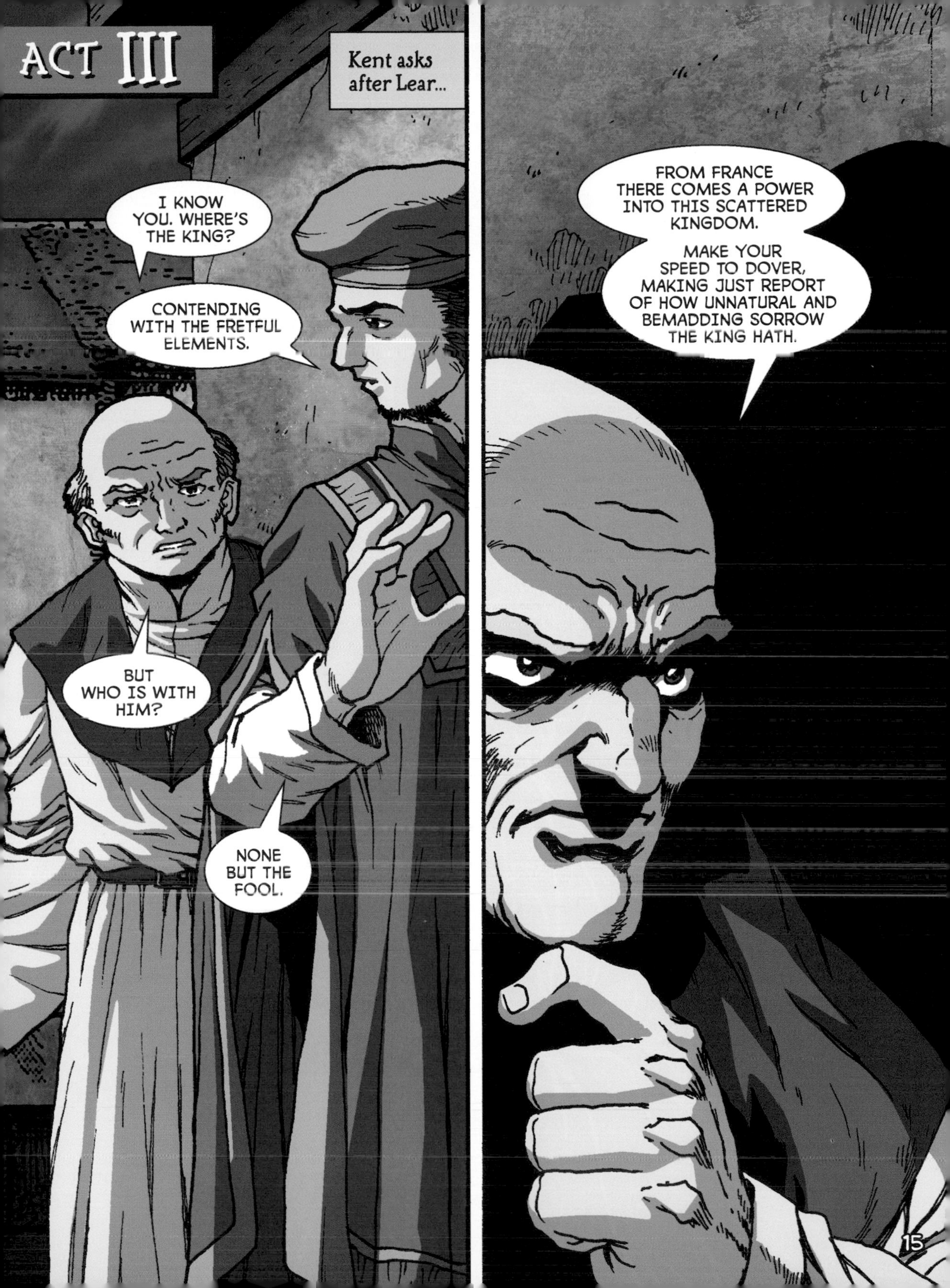
ACT III
Kent asks after Lear...
I KNOW YOU. WHERE'S THE KING?
CONTENDING WITH THE FRETFUL ELEMENTS.
BUT WHO IS WITH HIM?
NONE BUT THE FOOL.
FROM FRANCE THERE COMES A POWER INTO THIS SCATTERED KINGDOM.
MAKE YOUR SPEED TO DOVER, MAKING JUST REPORT OF HOW UNNATURAL AND BEMADDING SORROW THE KING HATH.

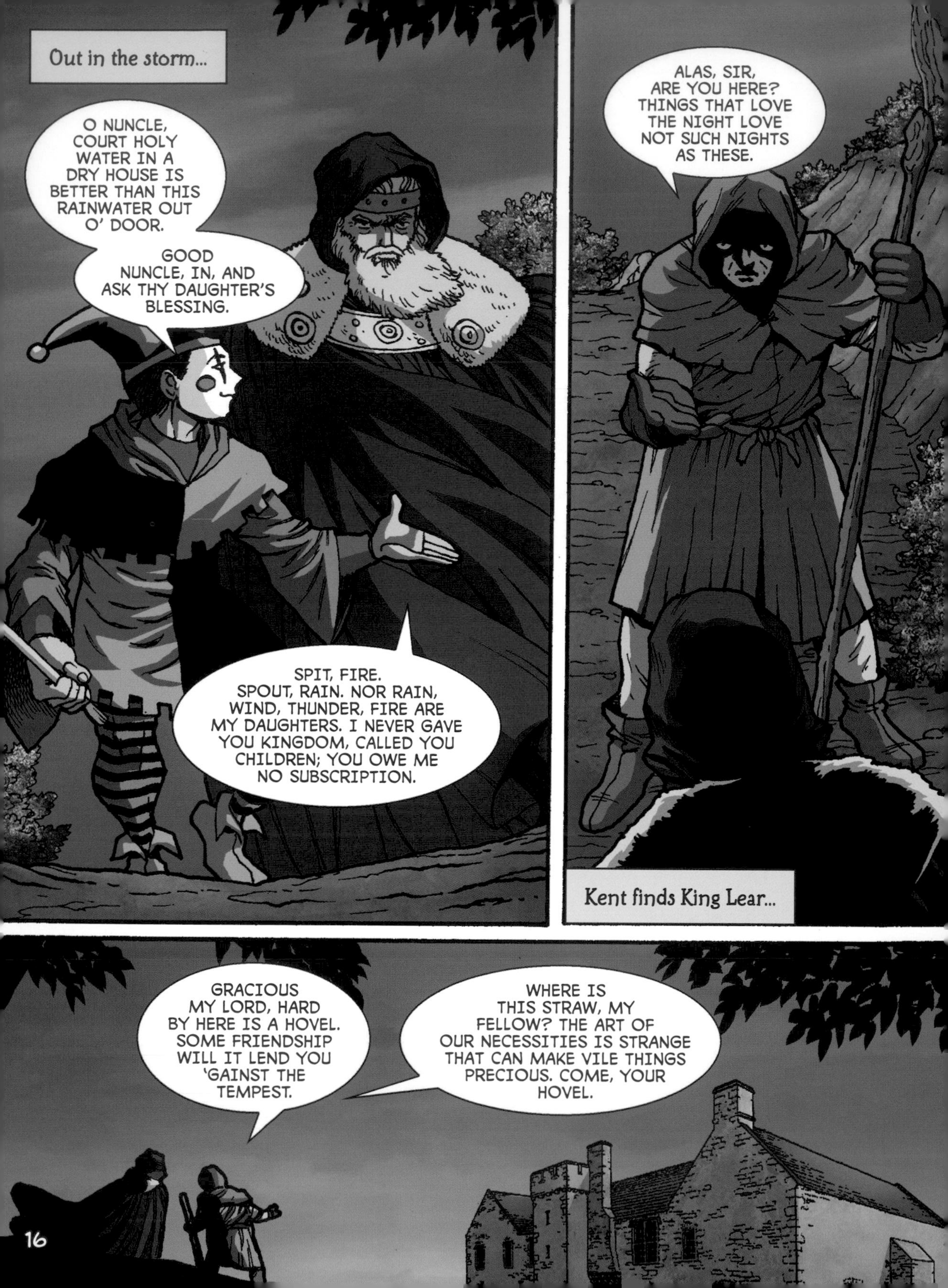
Out in the storm...
O NUNCLE, COURT HOLY WATER IN A DRY HOUSE IS BETTER THAN THIS RAINWATER OUT O' DOOR.
GOOD NUNCLE, IN, AND ASK THY DAUGHTER'S BLESSING.
SPIT, FIRE. SPOUT, RAIN. NOR RAIN, WIND, THUNDER, FIRE ARE MY DAUGHTERS. I NEVER GAVE YOU KINGDOM, CALLED YOU CHILDREN; YOU OWE ME NO SUBSCRIPTION.
ALAS, SIR, ARE YOU HERE? THINGS THAT LOVE THE NIGHT LOVE NOT SUCH NIGHTS AS THESE.
Kent finds King Lear...
GRACIOUS MY LORD, HARD BY HERE IS A HOVEL. SOME FRIENDSHIP WILL IT LEND YOU 'GAINST THE TEMPEST.
WHERE IS THIS STRAW, MY FELLOW? THE ART OF OUR NECESSITIES IS STRANGE THAT CAN MAKE VILE THINGS PRECIOUS. COME, YOUR HOVEL.

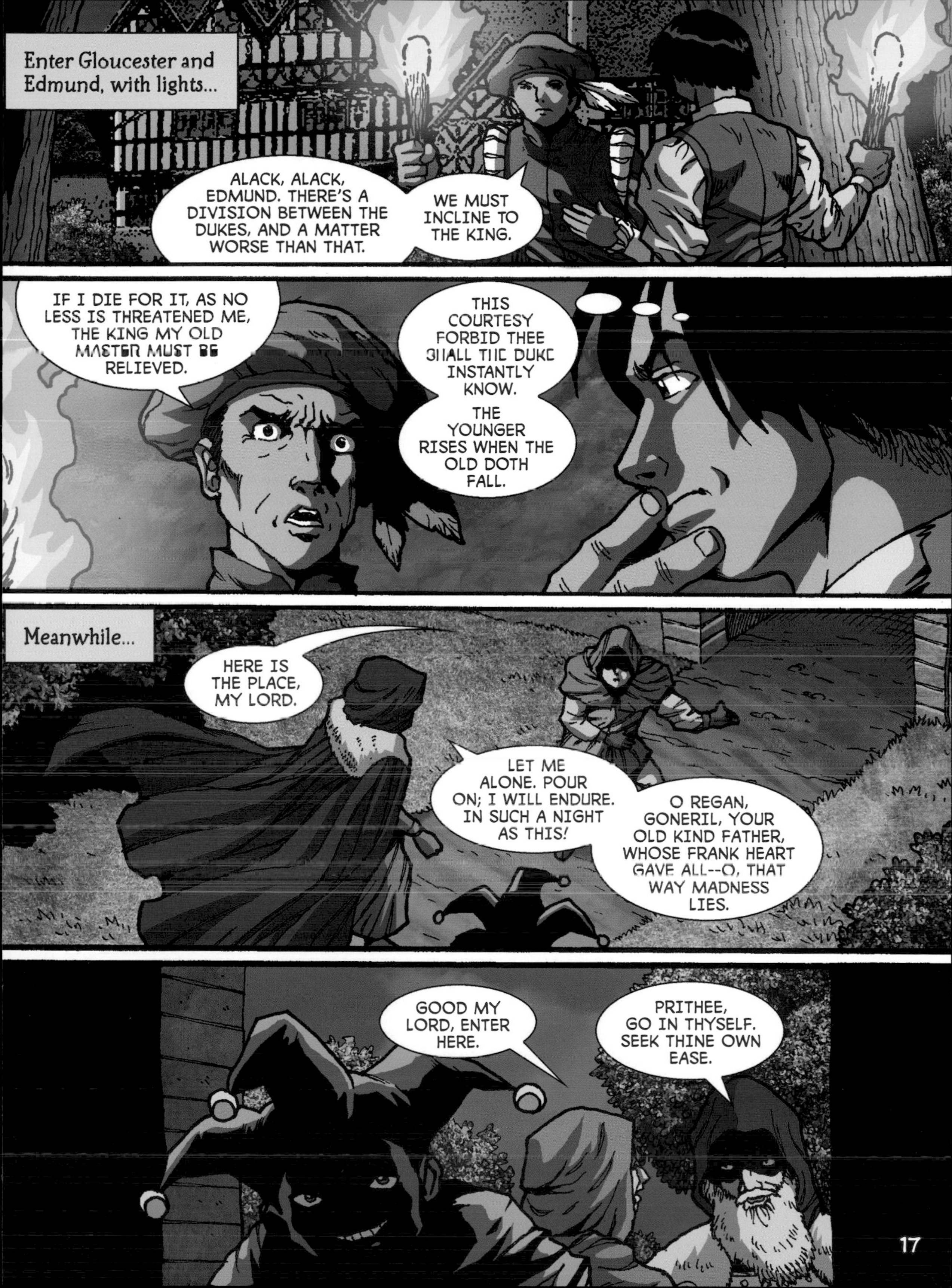
Enter Gloucester and Edmund, with lights...
ALACK, ALACK, EDMUND. THERE'S A DIVISION BETWEEN THE DUKES, AND A MATTER WORSE THAN THAT.
WE MUST INCLINE TO THE KING.
IF I DIE FOR IT, AS NO LESS IS THREATENED ME, THE KING MY OLD MASTER MUST BE RELIEVED.
THIS COURTESY FORBID THEE SHALL THE DUKE INSTANTLY KNOW.
THE YOUNGER RISES WHEN THE OLD DOTH FALL.
Meanwhile...
HERE IS THE PLACE, MY LORD.
LET ME ALONE. POUR ON; I WILL ENDURE. IN SUCH A NIGHT AS THIS!
O REGAN, GONERIL, YOUR OLD KIND FATHER, WHOSE FRANK HEART GAVE ALL--O, THAT WAY MADNESS LIES.
GOOD MY LORD, ENTER HERE.
PRITHEE, GO IN THYSELF. SEEK THINE OWN EASE.

18

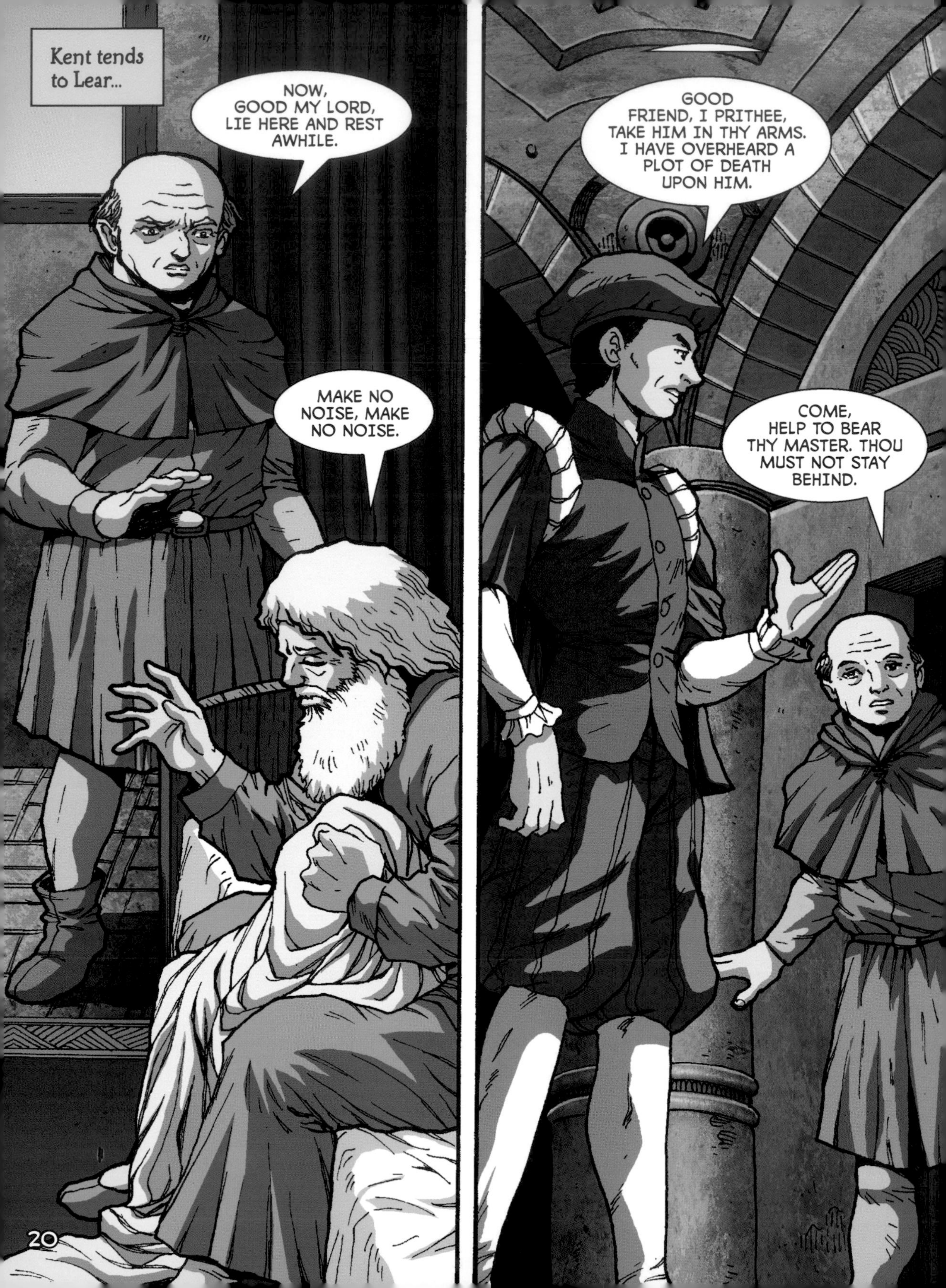

Kent tends to Lear...
NOW, GOOD MY LORD, LIE HERE AND REST AWHILE.
MAKE NO NOISE, MAKE NO NOISE.
GOOD FRIEND, I PRITHEE, TAKE HIM IN THY ARMS. I HAVE OVERHEARD A PLOT OF DEATH UPON HIM.
COME, HELP TO BEAR THY MASTER. THOU MUST NOT STAY BEHIND.

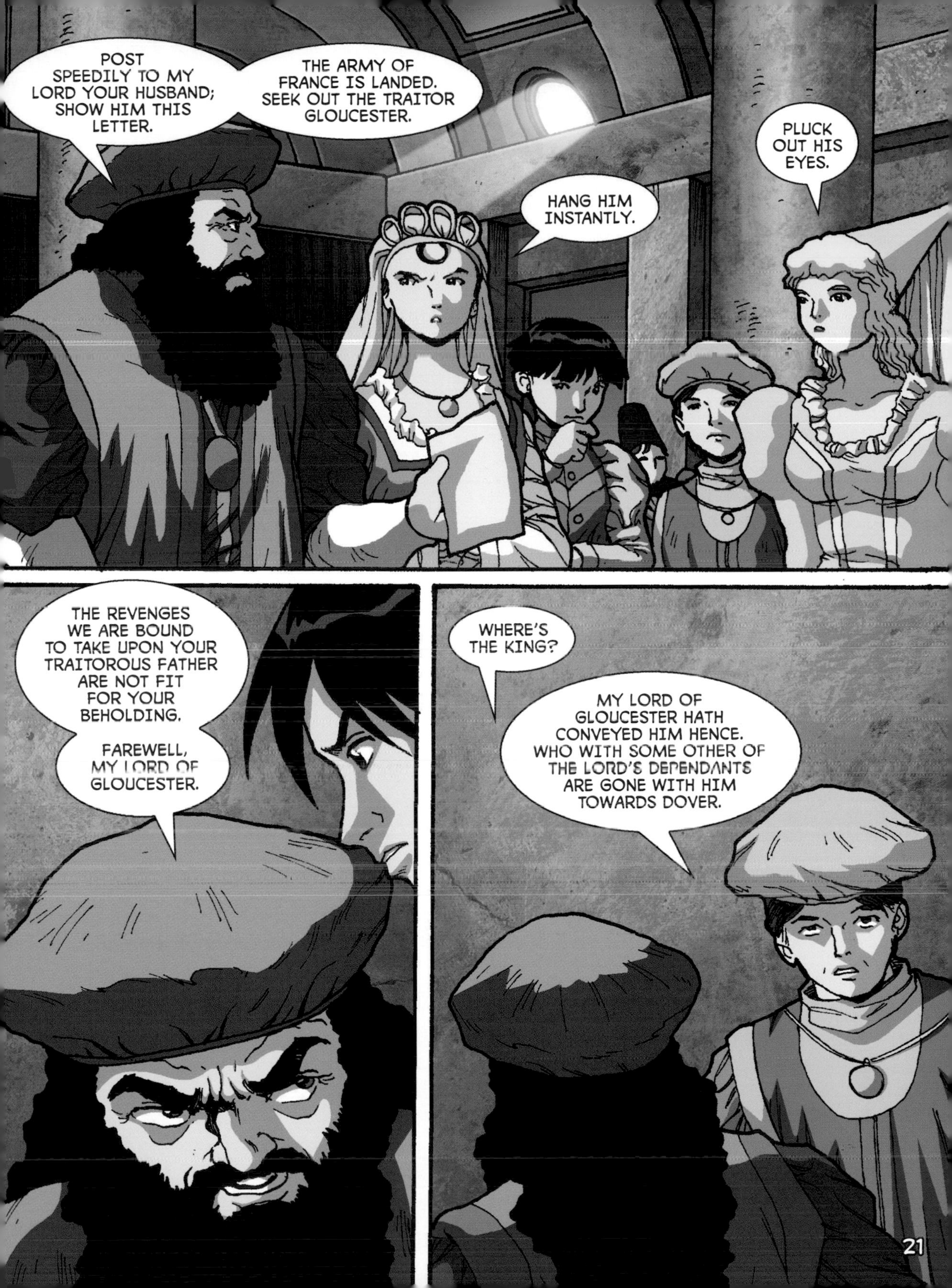
POST SPEEDILY TO MY LORD YOUR HUSBAND; SHOW HIM THIS LETTER.
THE ARMY OF FRANCE IS LANDED. SEEK OUT THE TRAITOR GLOUCESTER.
HANG HIM INSTANTLY.
PLUCK OUT HIS EYES.
THE REVENGES WE ARE BOUND TO TAKE UPON YOUR TRAITOROUS FATHER ARE NOT FIT FOR YOUR BEHOLDING.
FAREWELL, MY LORD OF GLOUCESTER.
WHERE'S THE KING?
MY LORD OF GLOUCESTER HATH CONVEYED HIM HENCE. WHO WITH SOME OTHER OF THE LORD'S DEPENDANTS ARE GONE WITH HIM TOWARDS DOVER.

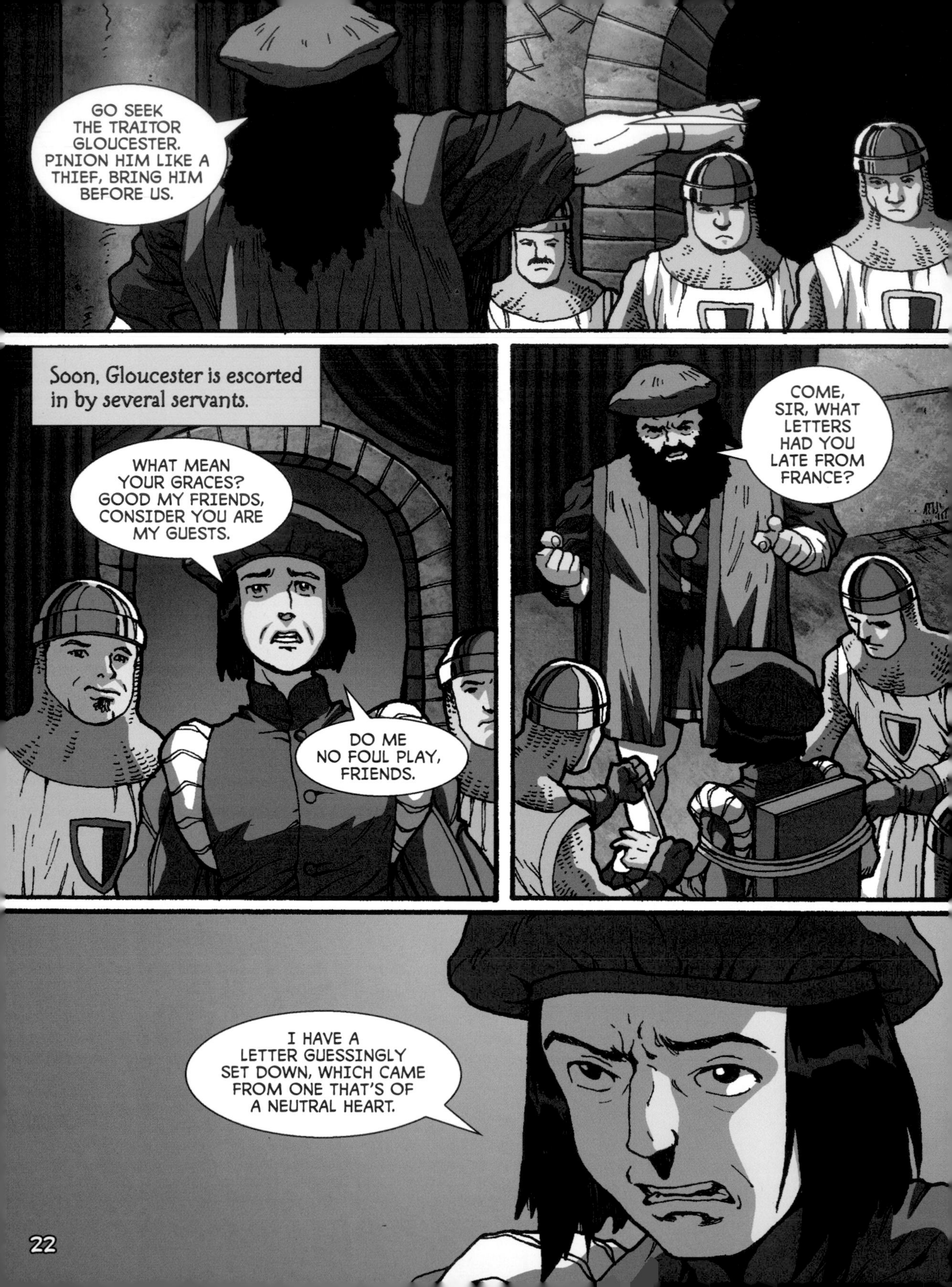

GO SEEK THE TRAITOR GLOUCESTER. PINION HIM LIKE A THIEF, BRING HIM BEFORE US.
Soon, Gloucester is escorted in by several servants.
WHAT MEAN YOUR GRACES? GOOD MY FRIENDS, CONSIDER YOU ARE MY GUESTS.
DO ME NO FOUL PLAY, FRIENDS.
COME, SIR, WHAT LETTERS HAD YOU LATE FROM FRANCE?
I HAVE A LETTER GUESSINGLY SET DOWN, WHICH CAME FROM ONE THAT'S OF A NEUTRAL HEART.

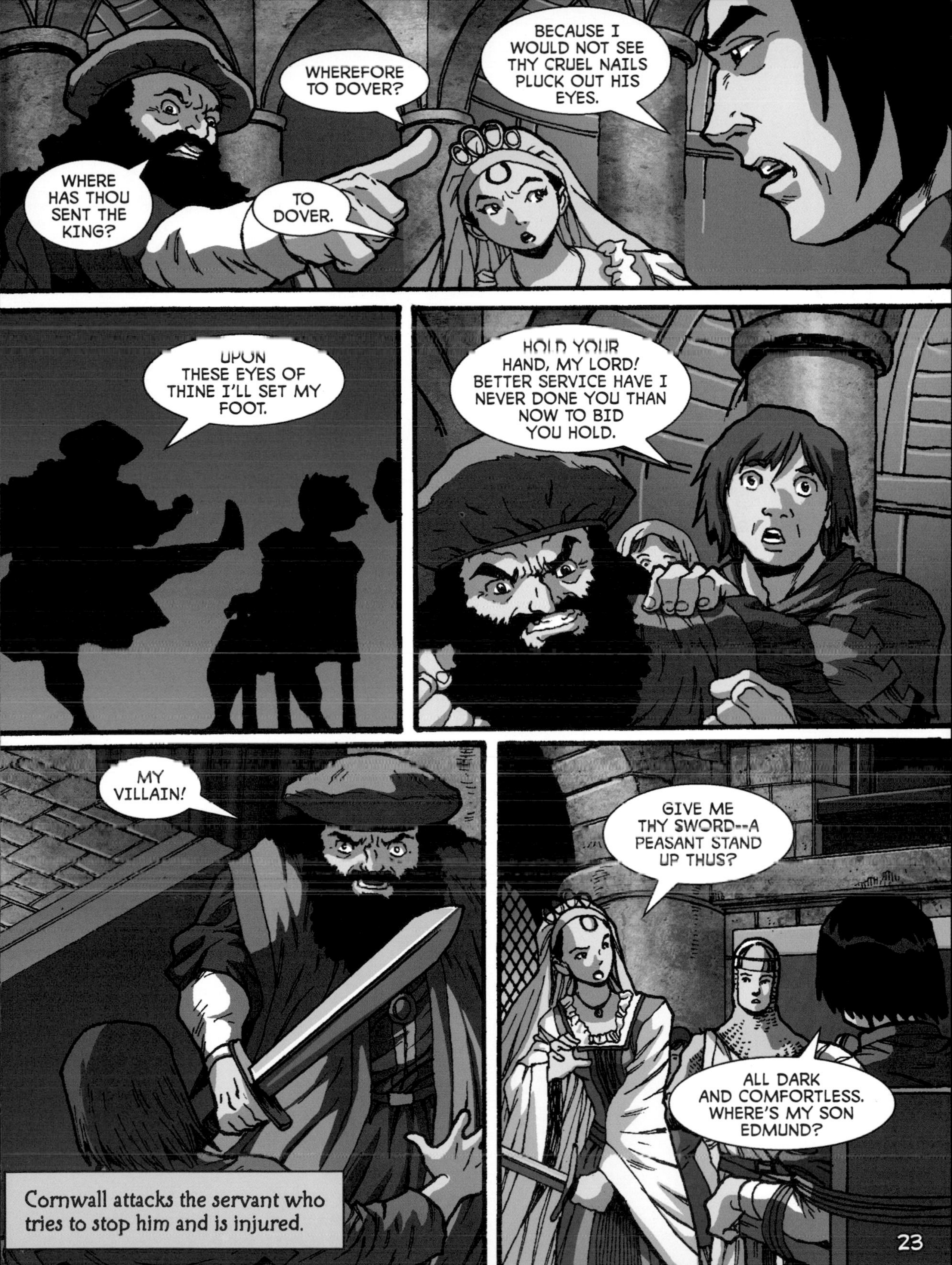
WHERE HAS THOU SENT THE KING?
TO DOVER.
WHEREFORE TO DOVER?
BECAUSE I WOULD NOT SEE THY CRUEL NAILS PLUCK OUT HIS EYES.
UPON THESE EYES OF THINE I'LL SET MY FOOT.
HOLD YOUR HAND, MY LORD! BETTER SERVICE HAVE I NEVER DONE YOU THAN NOW TO BID YOU HOLD.
MY VILLAIN!
Cornwall attacks the servant who tries to stop him and is injured.
GIVE ME THY SWORD--A PEASANT STAND UP THUS?
ALL DARK AND COMFORTLESS. WHERE'S MY SON EDMUND?

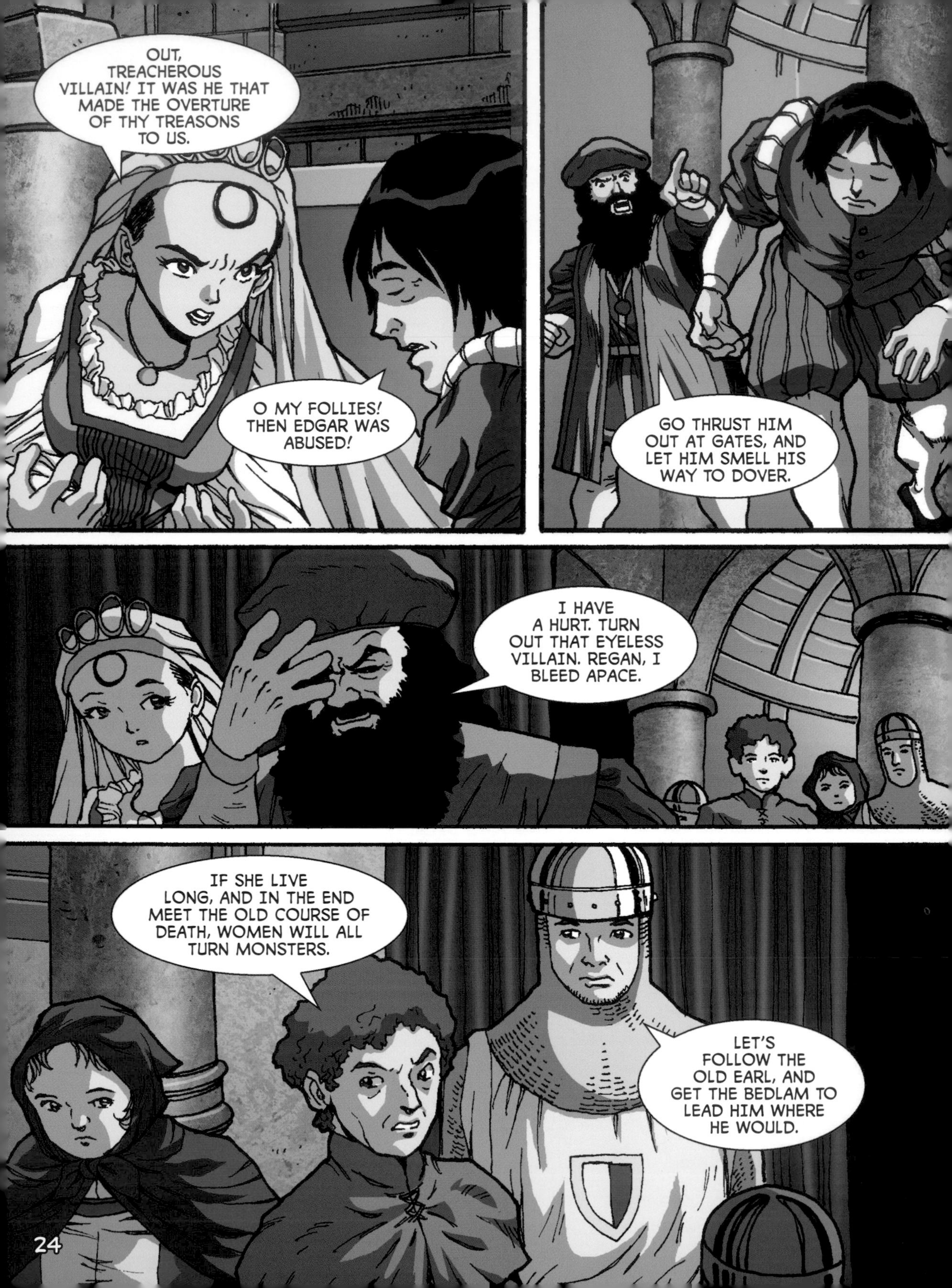
OUT, TREACHEROUS VILLAIN! IT WAS HE THAT MADE THE OVERTURE OF THY TREASONS TO US.
O MY FOLLIES! THEN EDGAR WAS ABUSED!
GO THRUST HIM OUT AT GATES, AND LET HIM SMELL HIS WAY TO DOVER.
I HAVE A HURT. TURN OUT THAT EYELESS VILLAIN. REGAN, I BLEED APACE.
IF SHE LIVE LONG, AND IN THE END MEET THE OLD COURSE OF DEATH, WOMEN WILL ALL TURN MONSTERS.
LET'S FOLLOW THE OLD EARL, AND GET THE BEDLAM TO LEAD HIM WHERE HE WOULD.

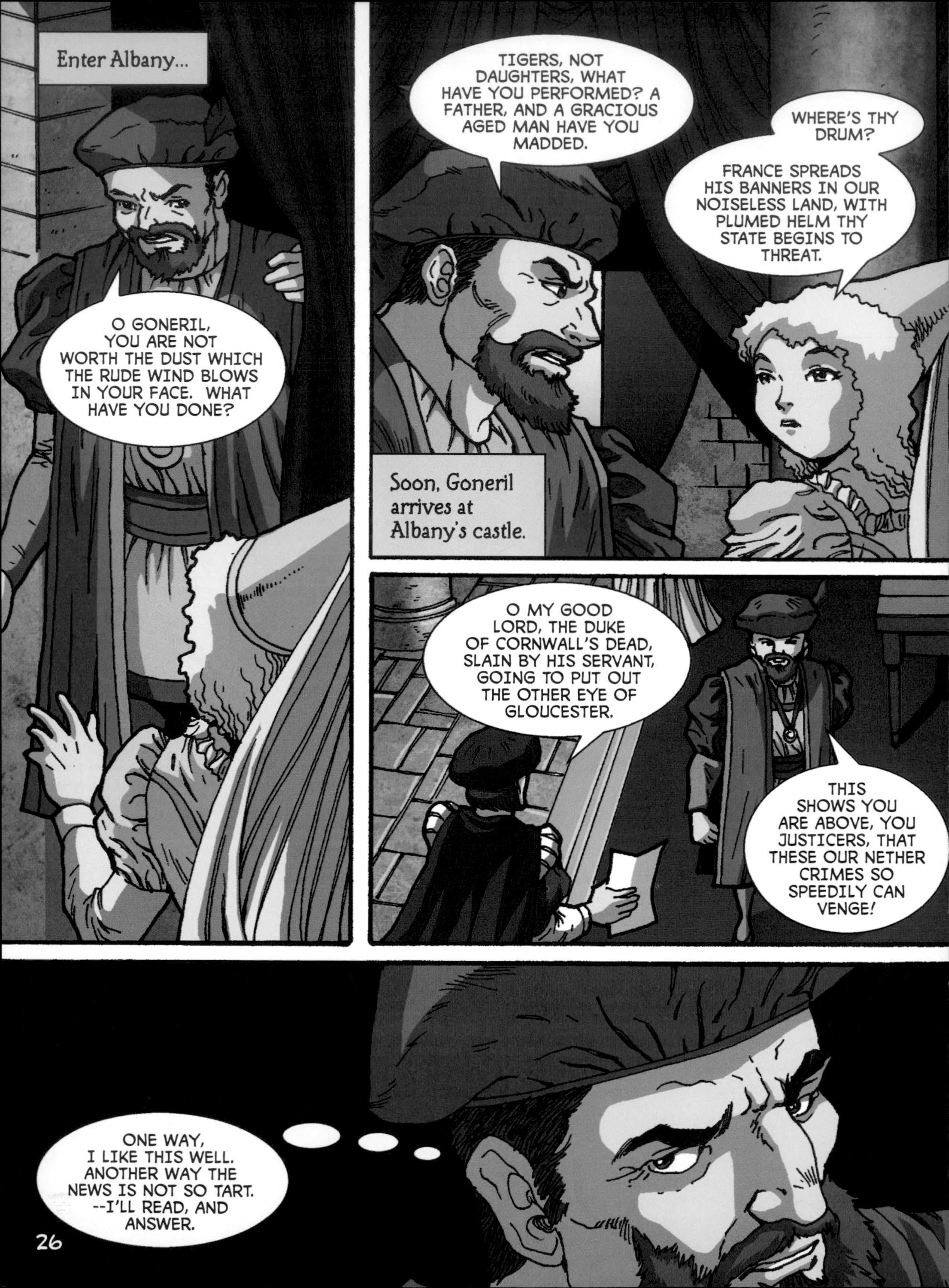
Enter Albany...
O GONERIL, YOU ARE NOT WORTH THE DUST WHICH THE RUDE WIND BLOWS IN YOUR FACE. WHAT HAVE YOU DONE?
Soon, Goneril arrives at Albany's castle.
TIGERS, NOT DAUGHTERS, WHAT HAVE YOU PERFORMED? A FATHER, AND A GRACIOUS AGED MAN HAVE YOU MADDED.
WHERE'S THY DRUM?
FRANCE SPREADS HIS BANNERS IN OUR NOISELESS LAND, WITH PLUMED HELM THY STATE BEGINS TO THREAT.
O MY GOOD LORD, THE DUKE OF CORNWALL'S DEAD, SLAIN BY HIS SERVANT, GOING TO PUT OUT THE OTHER EYE OF GLOUCESTER.
THIS SHOWS YOU ARE ABOVE, YOU JUSTICERS, THAT THESE OUR NETHER CRIMES SO SPEEDILY CAN VENGE!
ONE WAY, I LIKE THIS WELL. ANOTHER WAY THE NEWS IS NOT SO TART. --I'LL READ, AND ANSWER.

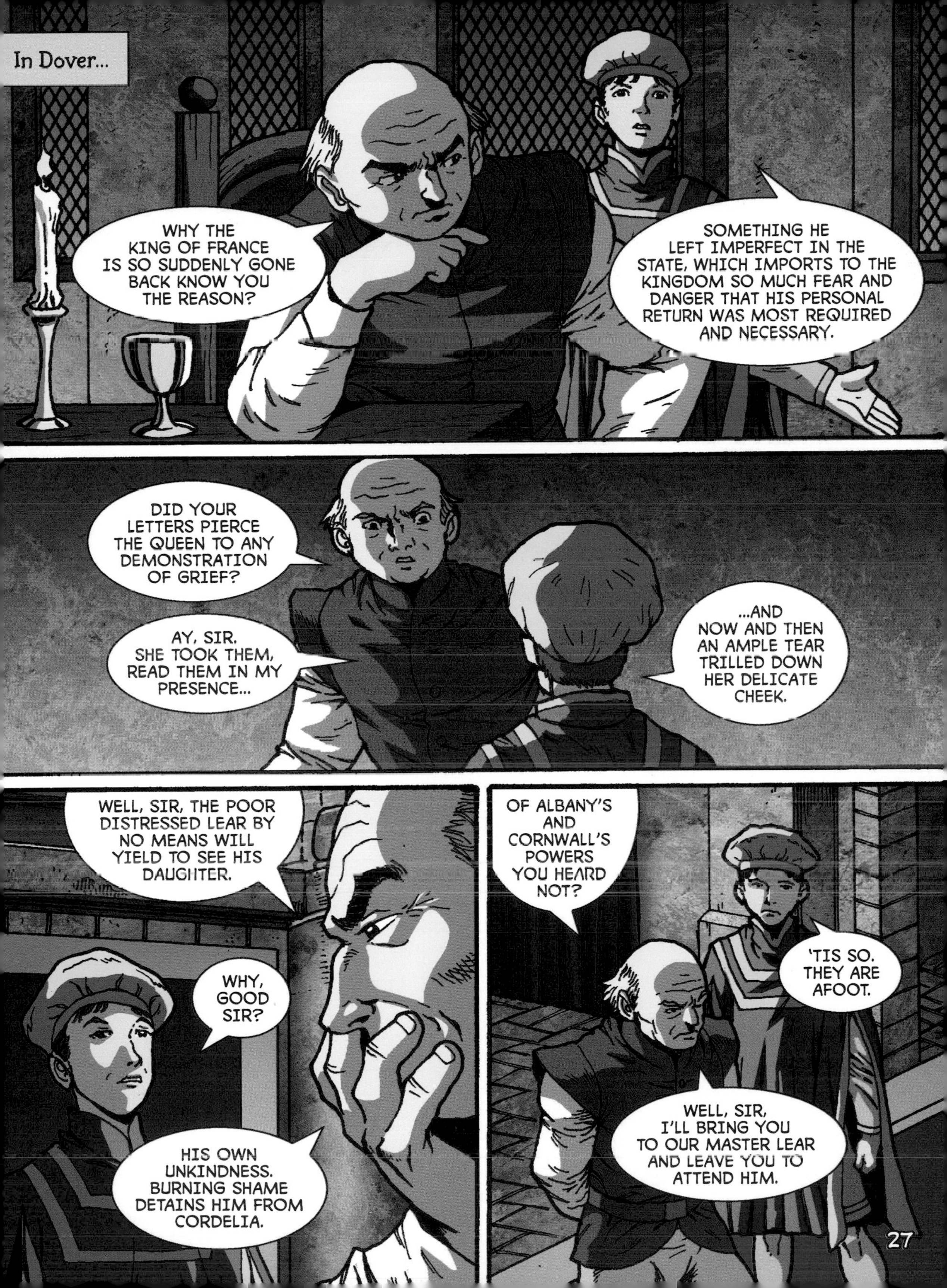
In Dover...
WHY THE KING OF FRANCE IS SO SUDDENLY GONE BACK KNOW YOU THE REASON?
SOMETHING HE LEFT IMPERFECT IN THE STATE, WHICH IMPORTS TO THE KINGDOM SO MUCH FEAR AND DANGER THAT HIS PERSONAL RETURN WAS MOST REQUIRED AND NECESSARY.
DID YOUR LETTERS PIERCE THE QUEEN TO ANY DEMONSTRATION OF GRIEF?
AY, SIR. SHE TOOK THEM, READ THEM IN MY PRESENCE...
...AND NOW AND THEN AN AMPLE TEAR TRILLED DOWN HER DELICATE CHEEK.
WELL, SIR, THE POOR DISTRESSED LEAR BY NO MEANS WILL YIELD TO SEE HIS DAUGHTER.
WHY, GOOD SIR?
HIS OWN UNKINDNESS. BURNING SHAME DETAINS HIM FROM CORDELIA.
OF ALBANY'S AND CORNWALL'S POWERS YOU HEARD NOT?
'TIS SO. THEY ARE AFOOT.
WELL, SIR, I'LL BRING YOU TO OUR MASTER LEAR AND LEAVE YOU TO ATTEND HIM.

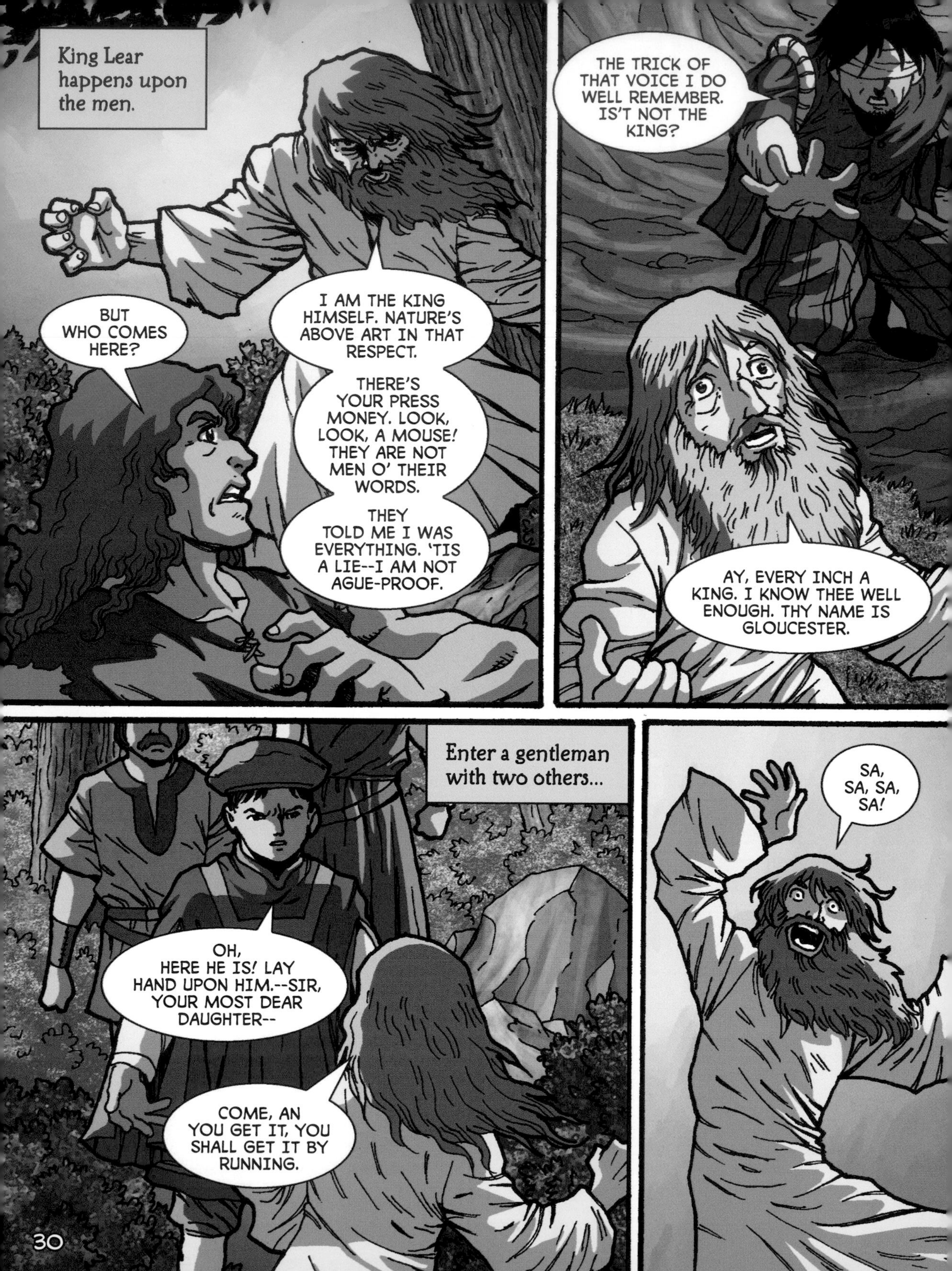
King Lear happens upon the men.
BUT WHO COMES HERE?
I AM THE KING HIMSELF. NATURE'S ABOVE ART IN THAT RESPECT.
THERE'S YOUR PRESS MONEY. LOOK, LOOK, A MOUSE! THEY ARE NOT MEN O' THEIR WORDS.
THEY TOLD ME I WAS EVERYTHING. 'TIS A LIE--I AM NOT AGUE-PROOF.
THE TRICK OF THAT VOICE I DO WELL REMEMBER. IS'T NOT THE KING?
AY, EVERY INCH A KING. I KNOW THEE WELL ENOUGH. THY NAME IS GLOUCESTER.
Enter a gentleman with two others...
OH, HERE HE IS! LAY HAND UPON HIM.--SIR, YOUR MOST DEAR DAUGHTER--
COME, AN YOU GET IT, YOU SHALL GET IT BY RUNNING.
SA, SA, SA, SA!

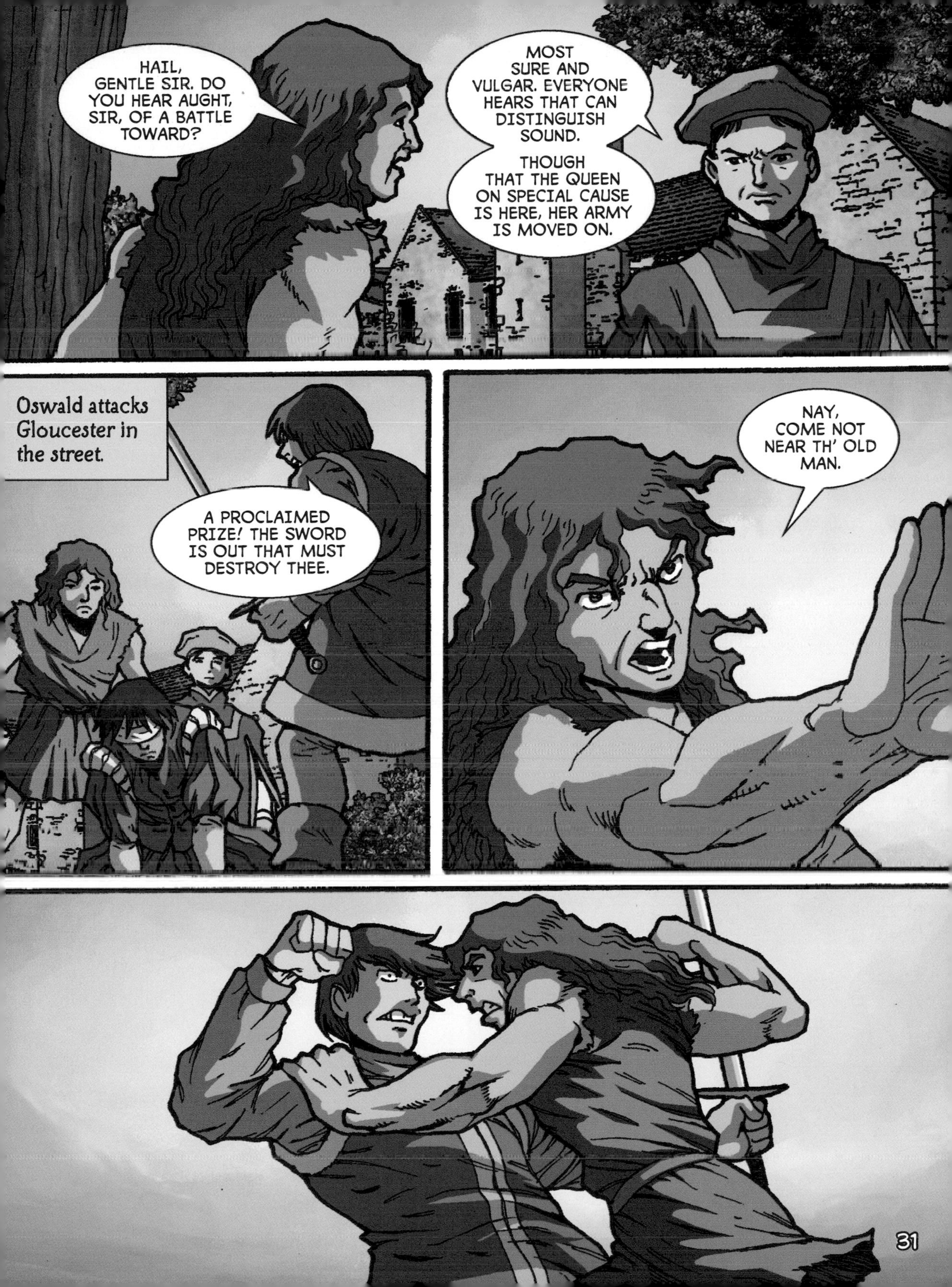
HAIL, GENTLE SIR. DO YOU HEAR AUGHT, SIR, OF A BATTLE TOWARD?
MOST SURE AND VULGAR. EVERYONE HEARS THAT CAN DISTINGUISH SOUND.
THOUGH THAT THE QUEEN ON SPECIAL CAUSE IS HERE, HER ARMY IS MOVED ON.
Oswald attacks Gloucester in the street.
A PROCLAIMED PRIZE! THE SWORD IS OUT THAT MUST DESTROY THEE.
NAY, COME NOT NEAR TH' OLD MAN.

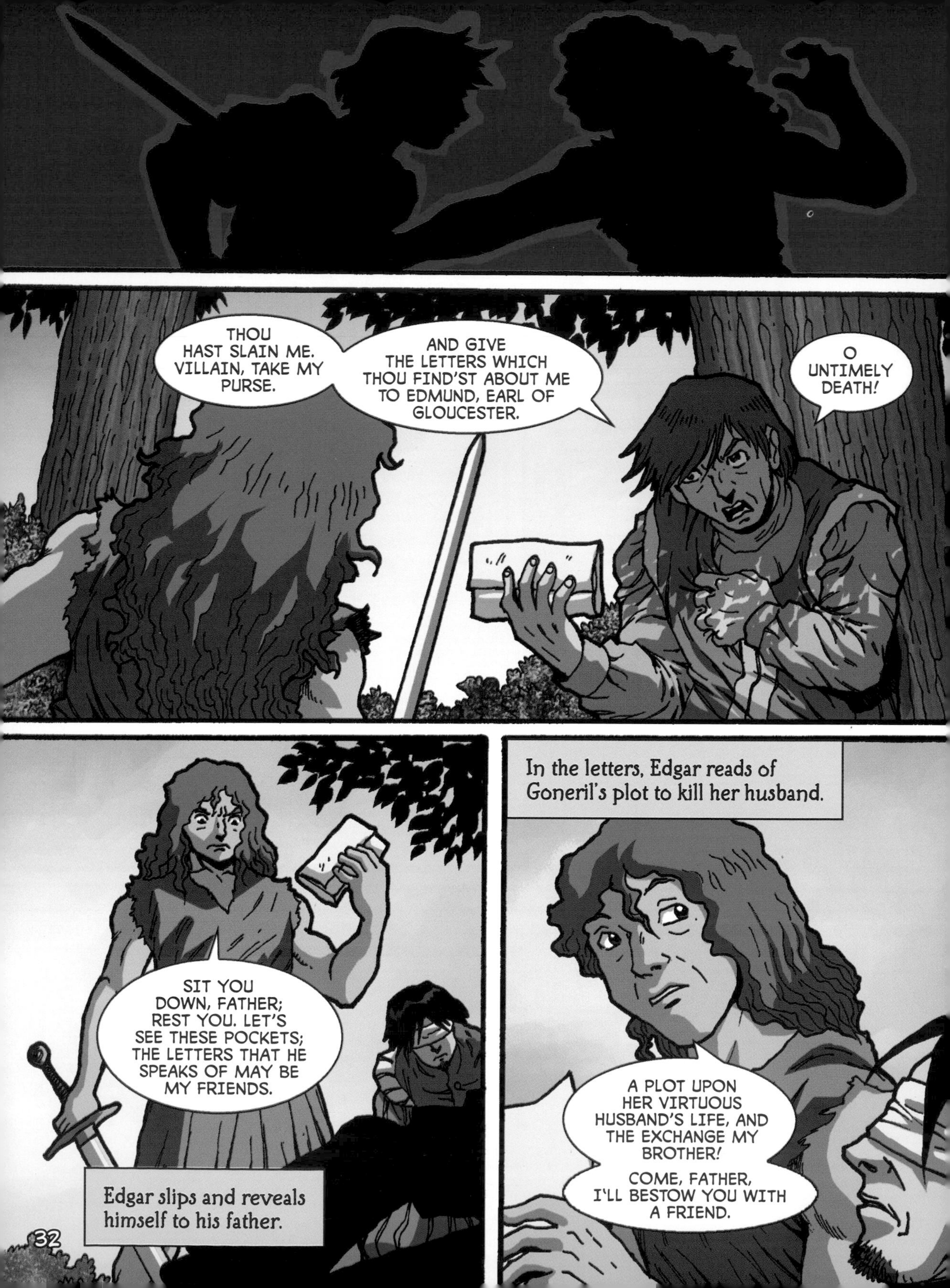
THOU HAST SLAIN ME. VILLAIN, TAKE MY PURSE.
AND GIVE THE LETTERS WHICH THOU FIND'ST ABOUT ME TO EDMUND, EARL OF GLOUCESTER.
O UNTIMELY DEATH!
SIT YOU DOWN, FATHER; REST YOU. LET'S SEE THESE POCKETS; THE LETTERS THAT HE SPEAKS OF MAY BE MY FRIENDS.
Edgar slips and reveals himself to his father.
In the letters, Edgar reads of Goneril's plot to kill her husband.
A PLOT UPON HER VIRTUOUS HUSBAND'S LIFE, AND THE EXCHANGE MY BROTHER!
COME, FATHER, I'LL BESTOW YOU WITH A FRIEND.

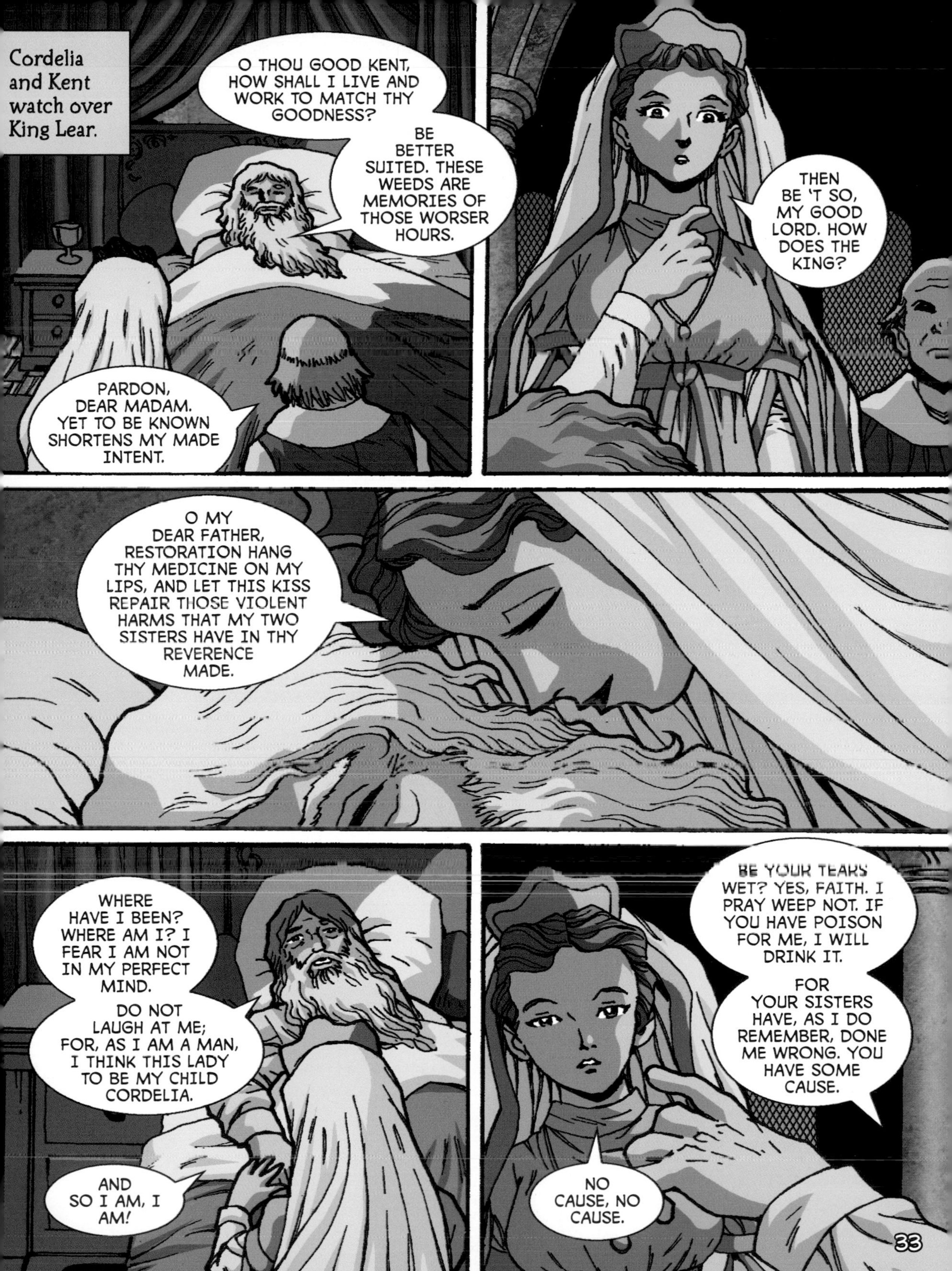

Cordelia and Kent watch over King Lear.
O THOU GOOD KENT, HOW SHALL I LIVE AND WORK TO MATCH THY GOODNESS?
BE BETTER SUITED. THESE WEEDS ARE MEMORIES OF THOSE WORSER HOURS.
PARDON, DEAR MADAM. YET TO BE KNOWN SHORTENS MY MADE INTENT.
THEN BE 'T SO, MY GOOD LORD. HOW DOES THE KING?
O MY DEAR FATHER, RESTORATION HANG THY MEDICINE ON MY LIPS, AND LET THIS KISS REPAIR THOSE VIOLENT HARMS THAT MY TWO SISTERS HAVE IN THY REVERENCE MADE.
WHERE HAVE I BEEN? WHERE AM I? I FEAR I AM NOT IN MY PERFECT MIND.
DO NOT LAUGH AT ME; FOR, AS I AM A MAN, I THINK THIS LADY TO BE MY CHILD CORDELIA.
AND SO I AM, I AM!
BE YOUR TEARS WET? YES, FAITH. I PRAY WEEP NOT. IF YOU HAVE POISON FOR ME, I WILL DRINK IT.
FOR YOUR SISTERS HAVE, AS I DO REMEMBER, DONE ME WRONG. YOU HAVE SOME CAUSE.
NO CAUSE, NO CAUSE.

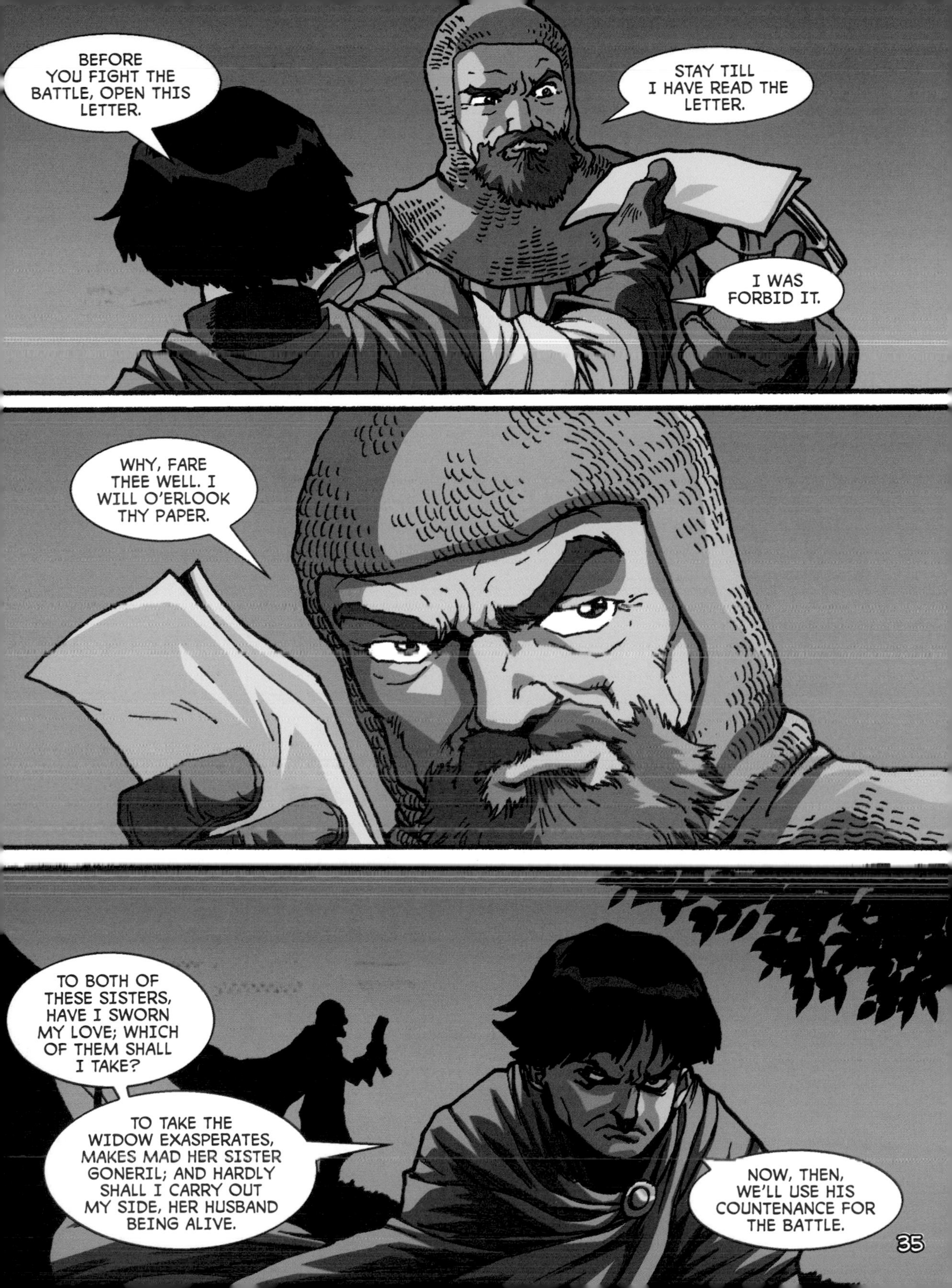
BEFORE YOU FIGHT THE BATTLE, OPEN THIS LETTER.
STAY TILL I HAVE READ THE LETTER.
I WAS FORBID IT.
WHY, FARE THEE WELL. I WILL O'ERLOOK THY PAPER.
TO BOTH OF THESE SISTERS, HAVE I SWORN MY LOVE; WHICH OF THEM SHALL I TAKE?
TO TAKE THE WIDOW EXASPERATES, MAKES MAD HER SISTER GONERIL; AND HARDLY SHALL I CARRY OUT MY SIDE, HER HUSBAND BEING ALIVE.
NOW, THEN, WE'LL USE HIS COUNTENANCE FOR THE BATTLE.

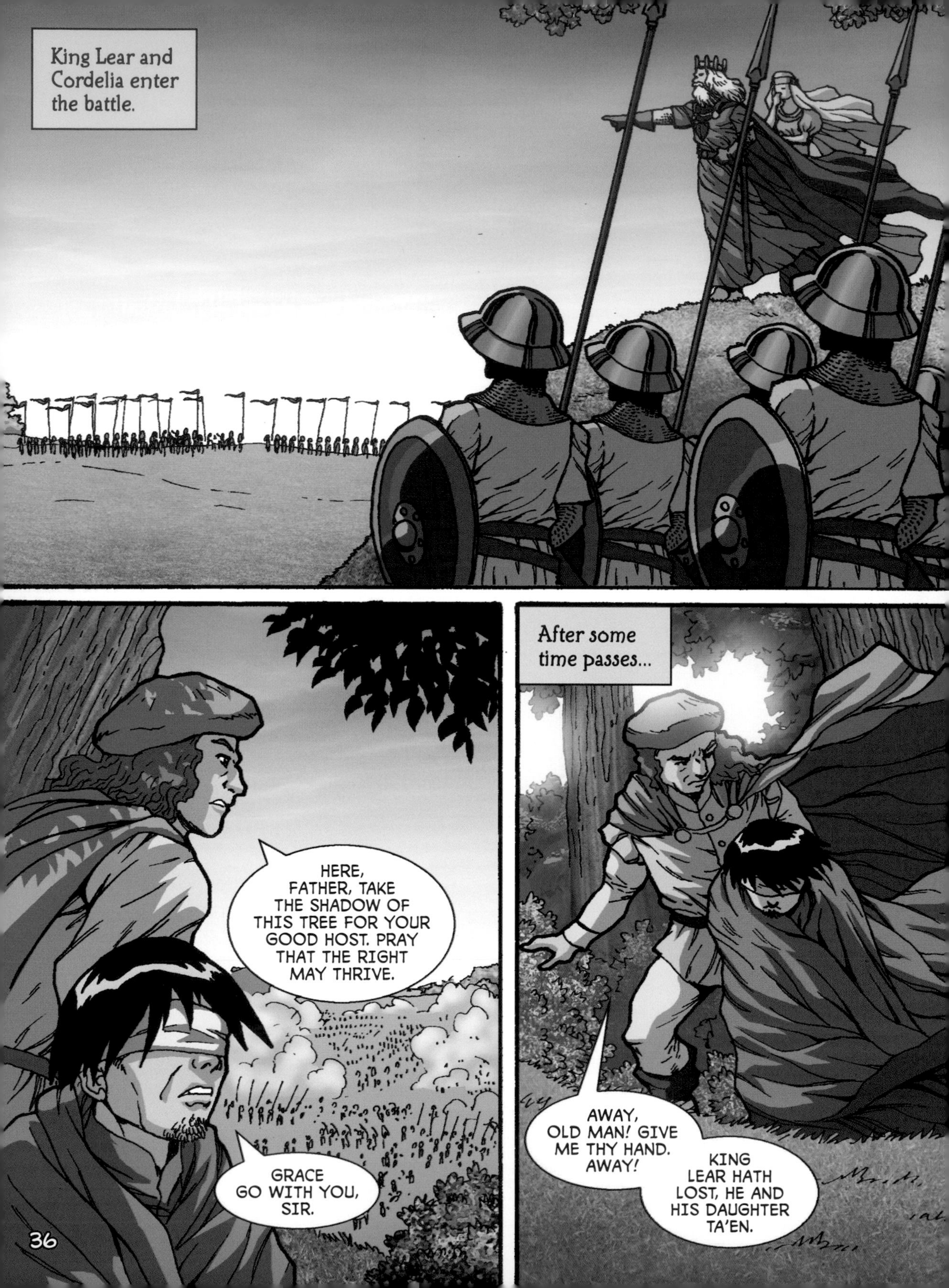
King Lear and Cordelia enter the battle.
HERE, FATHER, TAKE THE SHADOW OF THIS TREE FOR YOUR GOOD HOST. PRAY THAT THE RIGHT MAY THRIVE.
GRACE GO WITH YOU, SIR.
After some time passes...
AWAY, OLD MAN! GIVE ME THY HAND. AWAY!
KING LEAR HATH LOST, HE AND HIS DAUGHTER TA'EN.

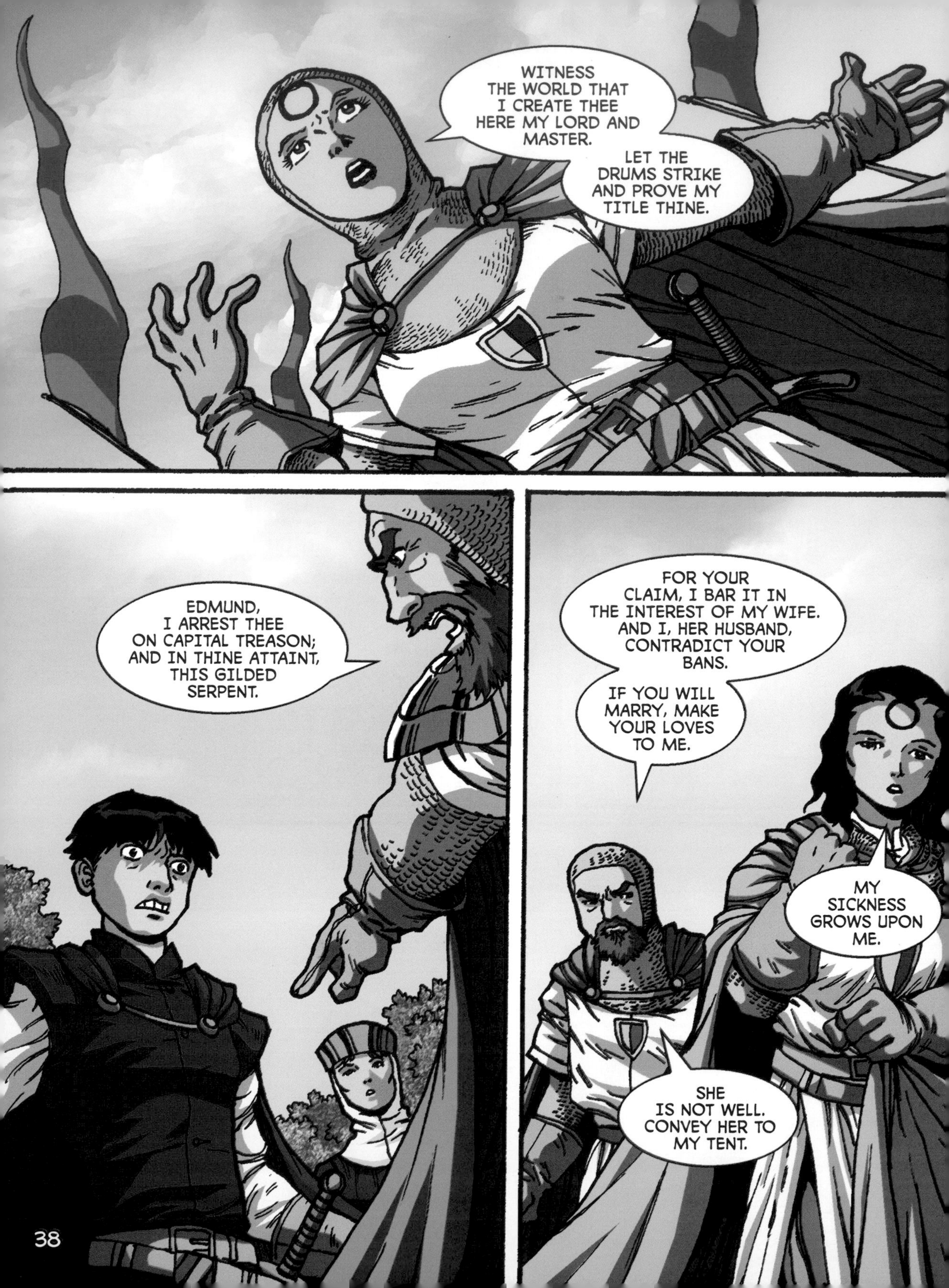
WITNESS THE WORLD THAT I CREATE THEE HERE MY LORD AND MASTER.
LET THE DRUMS STRIKE AND PROVE MY TITLE THINE.
EDMUND, I ARREST THEE ON CAPITAL TREASON; AND IN THINE ATTAINT, THIS GILDED SERPENT.
FOR YOUR CLAIM, I BAR IT IN THE INTEREST OF MY WIFE. AND I, HER HUSBAND, CONTRADICT YOUR BANS.
IF YOU WILL MARRY, MAKE YOUR LOVES TO ME.
MY SICKNESS GROWS UPON ME.
SHE IS NOT WELL. CONVEY HER TO MY TENT.

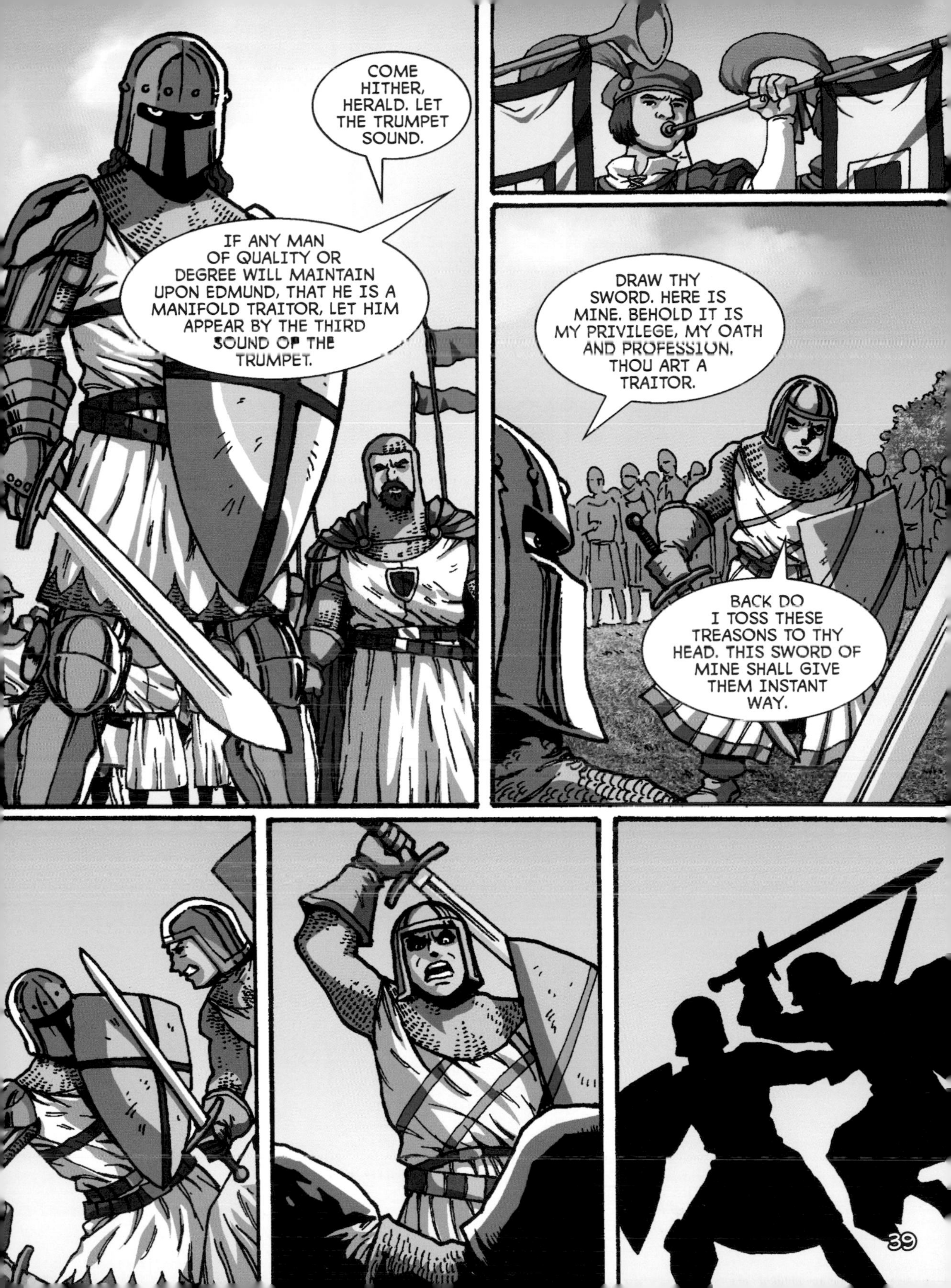
COME HITHER, HERALD. LET THE TRUMPET SOUND.
IF ANY MAN OF QUALITY OR DEGREE WILL MAINTAIN UPON EDMUND, THAT HE IS A MANIFOLD TRAITOR, LET HIM APPEAR BY THE THIRD SOUND OF THE TRUMPET.
DRAW THY SWORD. HERE IS MINE. BEHOLD IT IS MY PRIVILEGE, MY OATH AND PROFESSION. THOU ART A TRAITOR.
BACK DO I TOSS THESE TREASONS TO THY HEAD. THIS SWORD OF MINE SHALL GIVE THEM INSTANT WAY.

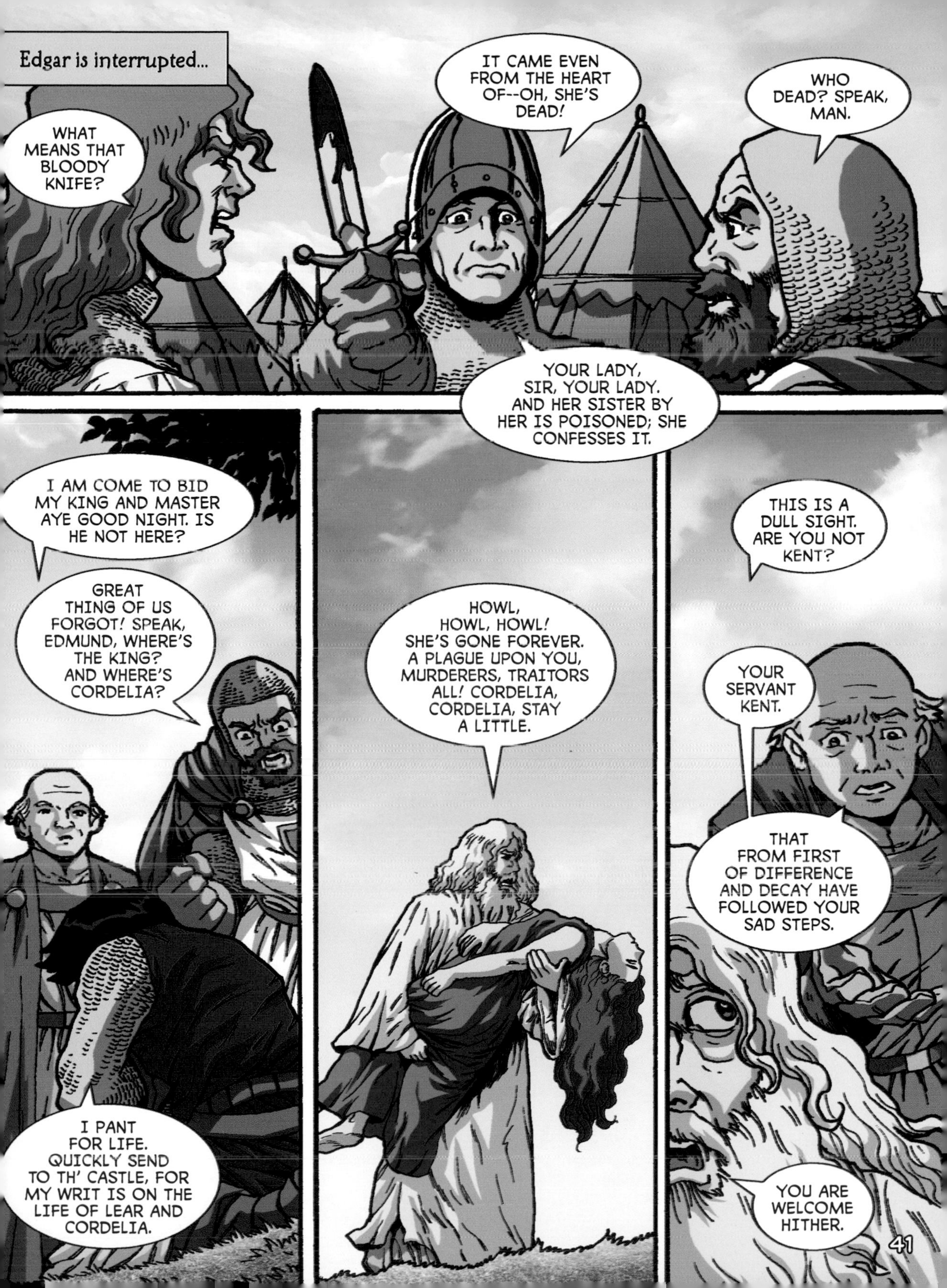
Edgar is interrupted...
WHAT MEANS THAT BLOODY KNIFE?
IT CAME EVEN FROM THE HEART OF--OH, SHE'S DEAD!
WHO DEAD? SPEAK, MAN.
YOUR LADY, SIR, YOUR LADY. AND HER SISTER BY HER IS POISONED; SHE CONFESSES IT.
I AM COME TO BID MY KING AND MASTER AYE GOOD NIGHT. IS HE NOT HERE?
GREAT THING OF US FORGOT! SPEAK, EDMUND, WHERE'S THE KING? AND WHERE'S CORDELIA?
I PANT FOR LIFE. QUICKLY SEND TO TH' CASTLE, FOR MY WRIT IS ON THE LIFE OF LEAR AND CORDELIA.
HOWL, HOWL, HOWL! SHE'S GONE FOREVER. A PLAGUE UPON YOU, MURDERERS, TRAITORS ALL! CORDELIA, CORDELIA, STAY A LITTLE.
THIS IS A DULL SIGHT. ARE YOU NOT KENT?
YOUR SERVANT KENT.
THAT FROM FIRST OF DIFFERENCE AND DECAY HAVE FOLLOWED YOUR SAD STEPS.
YOU ARE WELCOME HITHER.

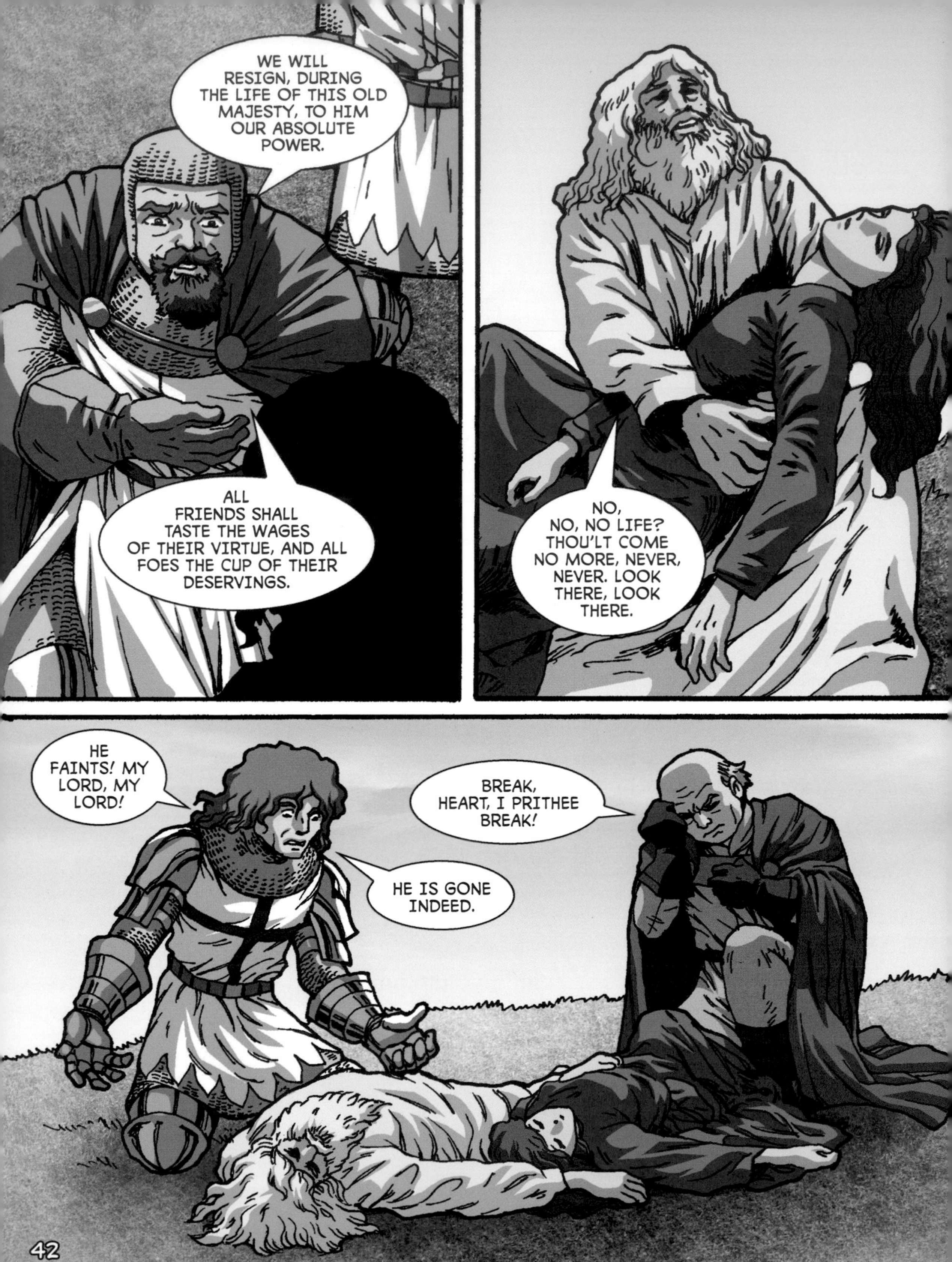
WE WILL RESIGN, DURING THE LIFE OF THIS OLD MAJESTY, TO HIM OUR ABSOLUTE POWER.
ALL FRIENDS SHALL TASTE THE WAGES OF THEIR VIRTUE, AND ALL FOES THE CUP OF THEIR DESERVINGS.
NO, NO, NO LIFE? THOU'LT COME NO MORE, NEVER, NEVER. LOOK THERE, LOOK THERE.
HE FAINTS! MY LORD, MY LORD!
BREAK, HEART, I PRITHEE BREAK!
HE IS GONE INDEED.

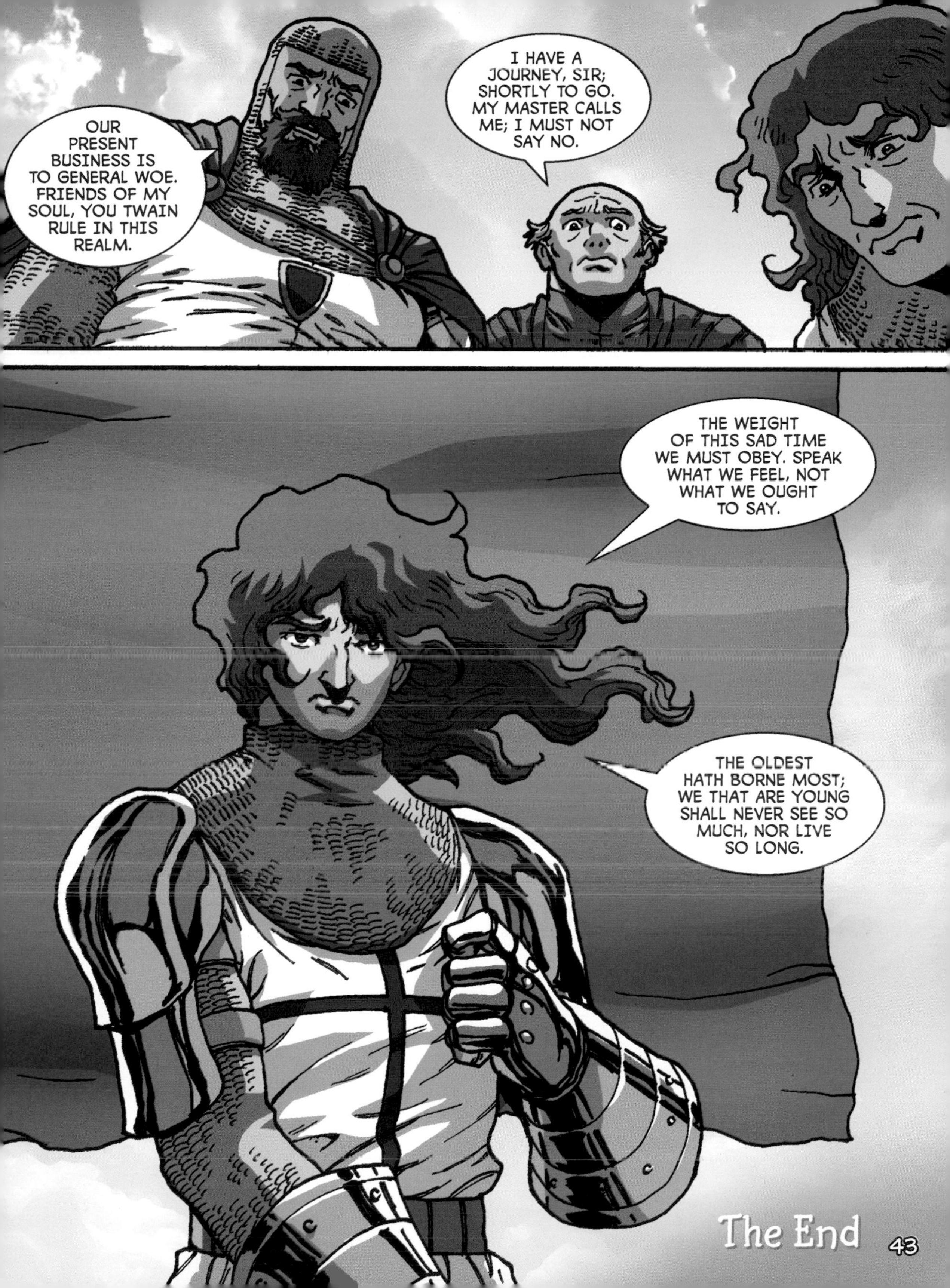
OUR PRESENT BUSINESS IS TO GENERAL WOE. FRIENDS OF MY SOUL, YOU TWAIN RULE IN THIS REALM.
I HAVE A JOURNEY, SIR; SHORTLY TO GO. MY MASTER CALLS ME; I MUST NOT SAY NO.
THE WEIGHT OF THIS SAD TIME WE MUST OBEY. SPEAK WHAT WE FEEL, NOT WHAT WE OUGHT TO SAY.
THE OLDEST HATH BORNE MOST; WE THAT ARE YOUNG SHALL NEVER SEE SO MUCH, NOR LIVE SO LONG.
The End

Discussion Questions

1. Do you think King Lear made the right decision in how to divide his property? Why or why not? What would you have done?

2. Cordelia chooses not to exaggerate her love for her father as her sisters did. Do you think that was a good decision? Why or why not? If she had done so, how might the actions of King Lear have been different?

3. King Lear seems to be a victim of circumstances. In what ways does he contribute to his experiences?

4. Who are the villains in the play? Is their fate different from the characters who may be considered good? What can you conclude about that?

5. King Lear is a tragedy play, and Lear is the tragic hero. What is Lear's tragic flaw?

Fun Facts

- *King Lear* is the only one of Shakespeare's tragedy plays to have two similar, entwined plots.
- King James I was the first king for whom King Lear was performed.
- *King Lear* has more references to animals and nature that any other of Shakespeare's plays.
- The name Cordelia is of Latin origin. It means *heart*.
- *King Lear* contains one of only two references to soccer in all of Shakespeare's plays. The other is in *The Comedy of Errors*.

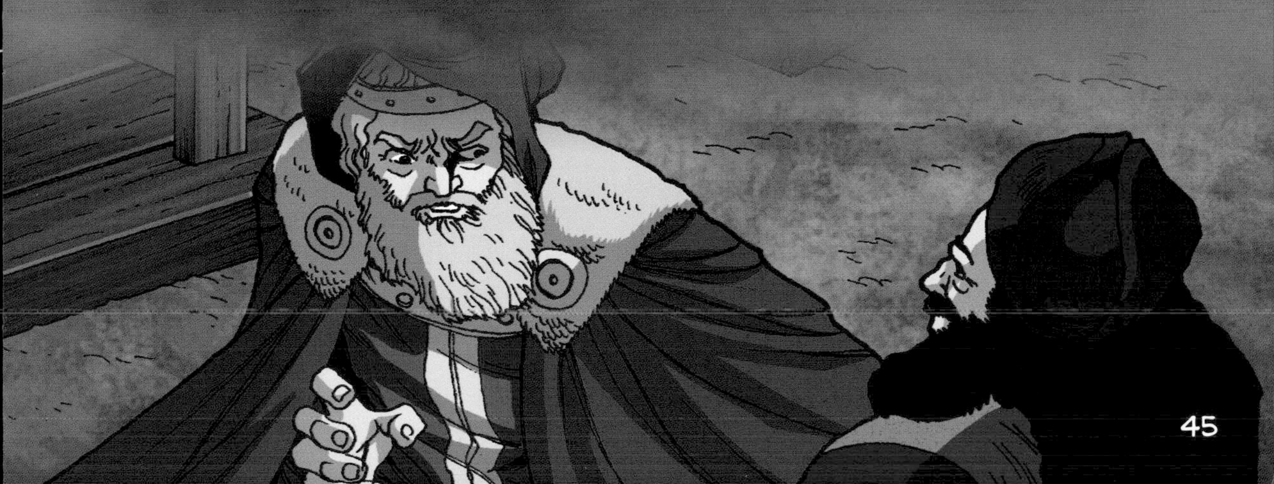

About Shakespeare

Records show William Shakespeare was baptized at Holy Trinity Church in Stratford-upon-Avon, England, on April 26, 1564. There were few birth records at the time, but Shakespeare's birthday is commonly recognized as April 23 of that year. His middle-class parents were John Shakespeare and Mary Arden. John was a tradesman who made gloves.

William most likely went to grammar school, but he did not go to university. He married Anne Hathaway in 1582, and they had three children: Susanna and twins Hamnet and Judith. Shakespeare was in London by 1592 working as an actor and playwright. He began to stand out for his writing. Later in his career, he partly owned the Globe Theater in London, and he was known throughout England.

To mark Shakespeare and his colleagues' success, King James I (reigned 1603–1625) named their theater company King's Men—a great honor. Shakespeare returned to Stratford in his retirement and died April 23, 1616. He was 52 years old.

Famous Phrases

Be your tears wet?

The wheel is come full circle.

Things that love the night love not such nights as these.

'Tis strange that from their cold'st neglect my love should kindle to inflamed respect.

Glossary

abjure – to reject.

beseech – to beg.

bestow – to give a place to stay.

durst – to dare.

felicitate – made happy.

hag – a witch.

knave – a young fellow.

nuncle – a form of address from a fool to his master.

opulent – having a large estate or property.

prithee – a way to make a request.

sojourn – a temporary stay.

weed – clothing.

Additional Works by Shakespeare

Romeo and Juliet (1594–96)

A Midsummer Night's Dream (1595–96)

The Merchant of Venice (1596-97)

Much Ado About Nothing (1598–99)

Hamlet (1599–1601)

Twelfth Night (1600–02)

Othello (1603–04)

King Lear (1605–06)

Macbeth (1606–07)

The Tempest (1610-11)

• *Bold titles are available in this set of Shakespeare Illustrated Classics.*

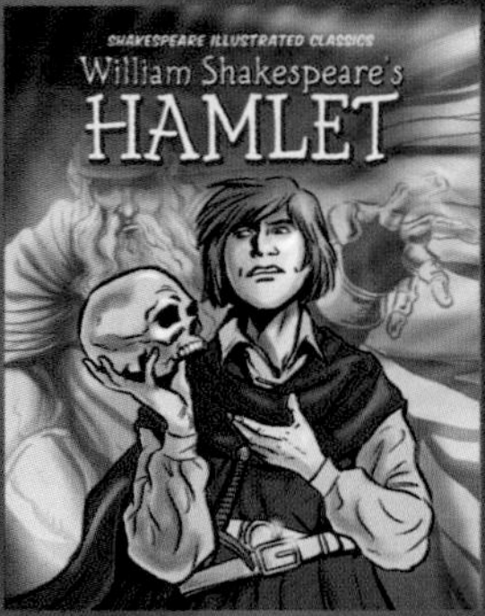
SHAKESPEARE ILLUSTRATED CLASSICS
William Shakespeare's
HAMLET

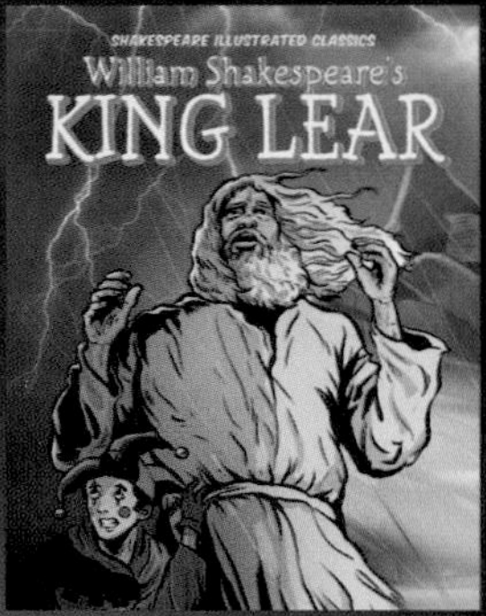
SHAKESPEARE ILLUSTRATED CLASSICS
William Shakespeare's
KING LEAR

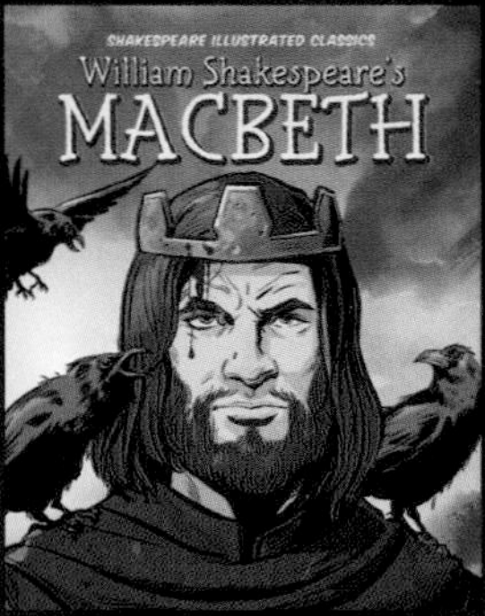
SHAKESPEARE ILLUSTRATED CLASSICS
William Shakespeare's
MACBETH

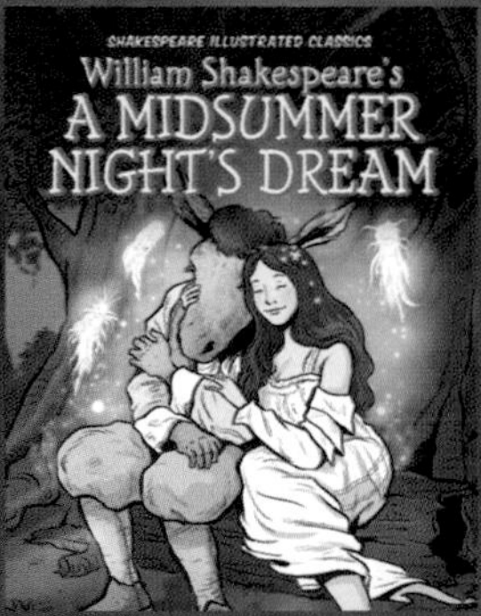
SHAKESPEARE ILLUSTRATED CLASSICS
William Shakespeare's
A MIDSUMMER NIGHT'S DREAM

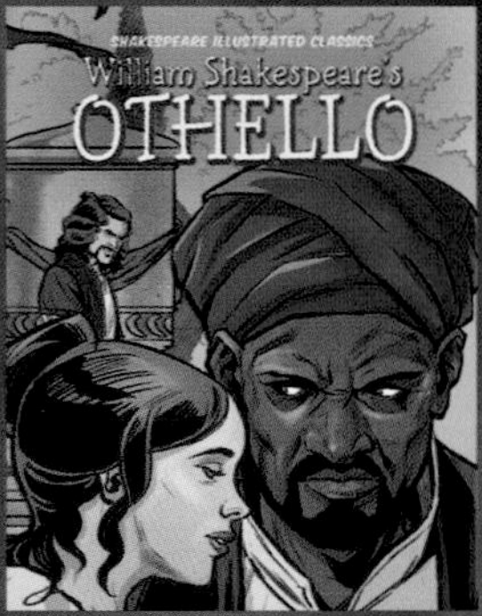
SHAKESPEARE ILLUSTRATED CLASSICS
William Shakespeare's
OTHELLO

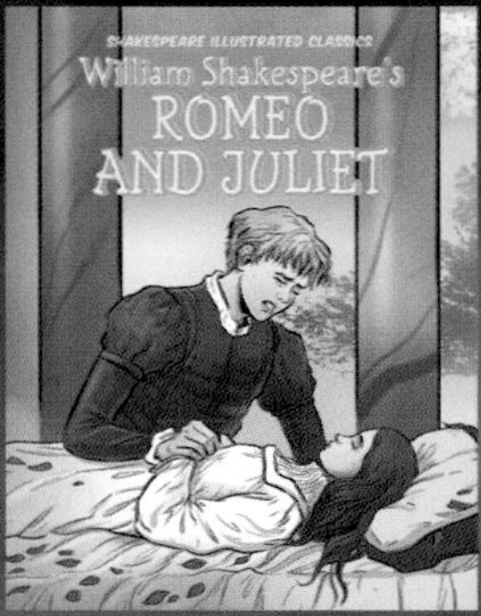
SHAKESPEARE ILLUSTRATED CLASSICS
William Shakespeare's
ROMEO AND JULIET